I0524213

DIANE E. TATUM

Main Street Mysteries #2:

Gemini Conspiracy

by

Diane E. Tatum

Review from Lisa Lickel

The Three Musketeers are on the case, keeping Daelin Georgia safe from crime, even if it's all the family. Captain Riley McDonough's world turns upside down in this new Main Street Mystery as secrets come to light in the midst of losses and gains. Soon the gang learns that good friends are worth their weight in gold, and the familial ties that bind are not always through blood. Join Dorie, Ross, and Riley in this new thriller that sends them searching for answers in photographs from the past.

Review from Kay Cook

[*Gemini Conspiracy*] was a good read and I enjoyed it very much. Thanks for letting me be a reviewer.

Review from Joyce Hiebert

[Gemini Conspiracy] is a good engrossing story. … The plot is great and moves fast.

Dedicated to my husband, Ken, and my family.

Special thanks to all the first responders who help
keep us well and whole.

As iron sharpens iron, so one person sharpens
another. Proverbs 27:17 (NIV)

A friend loves at all times, and a brother is born for a
time of adversity. Proverbs 17:17 (NIV)

One who has unreliable friends soon comes to ruin,
but there is a friend who sticks closer than a brother.
Proverbs 18:24 (NIV)

Two are better than one, because they have a good
return for their labor:
If either of them falls down, one can help the other up.
But pity anyone who falls and has no one to help
them up.
Also, if two lie down together, they will keep
warm. But how can one keep warm alone?
Though one may be overpowered, two can defend
themselves.
A cord of three strands is not quickly broken.
Ecclesiastes 4:9-12 (NIV)

Bear with each other and forgive one another if any
of you has a grievance against someone. Forgive as the
Lord forgave you. Colossians 3:13 (NIV)

Chapter 1

Beginning a new case ...

J ava Joint was jumping this night. Funky music played on the old-time juke box. Strobing lights pulsed on a makeshift dance floor that no one ever used. Best coffee in town.

Dorie Hudson practically owned the table in the corner booth, her office away from the *Daelin Beacon* offices. She usually shared the space with her favorite nursery owner/forest ranger/fiancé Ross MacAvoy. Dorie closed her laptop. Tears ran down her cheeks. She closed her eyes in hopes the tears would stop.

"One café mocha, double shot. Hey, what's going on?" The barista, Angela, wrapped her arm around Dorie's neck. "What did Ross do now?"

Dorie took the napkin and wiped her eyes. "Oh, he's happy working for the Forestry Service in California. He says its temporary, but his emails say otherwise."

"At some time, he'll figure out that happiness in Georgia is better than trees."

Dorie nodded, and Angela went back to work. Dorie started keying in her latest article before deadline.

The Java Joint bell over the door jangled as a tall cop entered the coffee shop.

"Hey, Captain Riley! Espresso dark and black?" Angela had a gift of remembering every customer's regular order.

"You got it, Angela!" Riley wandered over to Dorie's table. "How goes it, Miss Dorie?"

Dorie looked up and finished wiping the tears off her face with a napkin. "Hey, Riley. Have a seat."

The thin man slipped into the booth. His gun clunked against the table. "Sorry 'bout that, I'm on break. Gotta get back to it after my espresso." Riley smiled. "You look like you've been crying, my girl."

Dorie smiled. "My girl?"

"Someone needs to take care of you while Ross is away. I'm taking you on. I'll watch after you."

Dorie laughed. "I'm a big girl. I normally don't need a bodyguard."

Angela brought Riley's steaming cup over. "Enjoy. Stay safe out there, Riley."

"There's hardly any crime in Daelin, at least until Miss Dorie came to town anyway."

Riley McDonough had become the Chief of Police in Daelin after the arrest and detainment of the previous captain who helped cover up a murder with the now former mayor. Both sat in jail, without bail, awaiting trial for aiding and abetting said murderer.

Riley's walkie squawked to life. "Break in at the Records office. Captain, you available?"

"Ten-four, Joe. I'll head over there." Riley shoved

the cup of espresso toward Dorie. "Have this on me. Just don't blame me if it keeps you up all night."

Dorie smiled. "No problem. I'll be up for a while anyway or until Angela kicks me out. Swing back through if you have time."

Riley nodded and headed for the door.

"Wait!" Dorie closed the laptop. "Can I follow you over?"

"For you, you can ride with me and run the lights and siren."

Dorie turned to pack up.

"Nah, leave it. I'll make sure it's okay, Dorie. Go, play cop." Angela waved her away. She handed Riley a to go cup with his espresso order.

"You're the best, Angie." Riley nodded to her then turned to Dorie. "Ready? Let's go nab us a bad guy."

Chapter 2

Getting stranger and stranger …

Daelin was a quiet community nestled in the north Georgia foothills. In the dark, it seemed unoccupied. It was hard to think that there would be crime here, except for the murder Dorie had uncovered with Ross, her fiancé. Now he was doing a six-month stint in California replanting trees in the National Forests, so he could get a job in Georgia as a ranger in the Chattahoochee Forest. Before he left for California, Ross had moved Dorie into his house on the mountain just outside Helen, GA.

As an investigative reporter, Dorie had never ridden in a police car. Riley ran the flashing lights without the siren, hoping to catch the thief in the act, breaking into the records office.

After Riley cleared the scene, he motioned for Dorie to come in. The glass in the door was broken, and the door stood open. Records were strewn over the floor. Dorie stepped gingerly over the scene.

Riley put on latex gloves and threw a pair at Dorie. He began checking the back door for evidence.

"Don't touch anything without gloves. Don't move anything until my crime scene detectives get pictures."

As though conjured, the forensic van pulled up outside.

"Riley, were you born here in Daelin?" Dorie examined the antiquated drawer system. Only one drawer had been disturbed: the records labeled 1990 Mac-Mc. "Why do you think the only drawer dumped is the one yours and Ross's birth records were in?"

Riley shrugged. "Can't imagine why. This looks like vandals. We'll get prints off the drawer and the entrance."

"Is it okay if I gather and sort these records?" Dorie pointed out the large index cards.

"Once the team has gathered evidence, knock yourself out. Just don't touch anything that the vandal touched in case we can get prints."

As the detective crime scene unit poured into the old building, Dorie's phone rang. Ross, on FaceTime.

"Hey, Ross. How are you?" Dorie wandered outside on the Main Street sidewalk to a wrought iron bench.

"Where are you? Downton Daelin?"

"At a crime scene with Riley. It's just a break-in, no death or intrigue."

Ross grinned. "You promised no policework while I'm gone, remember? I want to come home to you."

"I can't wait. We are both going to St. Louis for Thanksgiving, right?"

"Yes, sweetheart. To meet your family for the 'Hudson Family Seal of Approval.'" He laughed a deep, good-hearted laugh. "I'm marrying you regardless, you know."

Dorie couldn't help smiling. "How could they not love you?" She loved him, his sandy hair, deep blue eyes, red beard, and broad shoulders. If only he wasn't so far away. "After all, I do. That's what matters, isn't it?"

"It's what matters most to me, my love."

Riley appeared in the screen corner with Dorie. "Get a room, guys! You're going to make my detectives hurl."

"We're working on it, bro." Ross wangled his red-brown eyebrows. "What are you doing out with my girl?"

"You didn't say I couldn't take her out to crime scenes. After all, you're not here to entertain her."

Dorie stood and walked away from Riley. "Don't listen to him. He's just jealous of you."

"Growing up, he was always the one with the best toys though. About time I bested him in something." Ross sat on the edge of his motel bed. "Seriously, I tried you at home on our video call system. I was worried when you weren't home."

"I was trying to finish an article at Java Joint. Then Riley got this call, and I figured it could be interesting. Your birthday's in 1990 too, isn't it?"

"Don't remind me. Turning thirty soon enough." He smiled. "And yes, I know I'm marrying a child. Twenty-three in January, right?"

"The only drawer dumped was 1990, Mac-Mc." Dorie smiled. "I miss you."

"I miss you, too. I'll see you in about seven weeks in St. Louie, Louie." He threw her a kiss.

"Seven weeks." She threw him a kiss back. Then he hung up.

Dorie walked back to the Records Office and waited until Riley said it was okay to come in. She found an empty box in the recycling bin outside to sort the jumbled records in. Dorie sat on the bench while the crime scene personnel began dusting for prints, taking photos, and inspecting the scene for any blood evidence around the broken glass.

After hours of noisy, focused business, the records office began to quiet. The crime scene specialists hauled their samples, cameras, and cases out to the van. Riley and Dorie were the only ones still on the scene.

"Come on in. You can gather up the cards. See if you can determine if anything's missing."

Dorie began sorting the cards into numerical order by birthdate. She lingered over Ross MacAvoy's birth record. *Should I or shouldn't I? Hmmm. If I plan to marry him, I should know all I can.* Dorie quickly copied the card as Riley gave last minute instructions to the forensics squad and talked to the county clerk. As he entered, Dorie jammed the page into her pocket, slipping the card from the copier glass.

"How goes it, Dorie?" Riley sat down across the table from her. "Anything missing?"

"Actually, yes. Two cards are missing as far as I can tell. All the cards are numbered sequentially. When were you born, Riley?"

"May 28, 1990."

Dorie made her puzzled face. "That's what I guessed because yours is one of the cards missing. The other one is the same day with a last name that starts with Mc. Know anyone with the same birthday?"

Riley shrugged. "No, I don't guess so. It could be someone who has moved away."

"Why would someone take your birth card and the one closest to it? Do you have a twin? May 28 is in the sign of Gemini, you know."

Riley laughed. "I think Mama would have told me something like that. Still it's a little creepy. If you write a story about this, you should leave out those details for now."

Dorie nodded and stripped off her sweaty latex gloves.

The first rays of sun crept over the mountain.

"Could you drop me by the Java Joint? I've got to pick up my stuff and my car. Maybe I can grab a couple hours sleep before showing up at the *Beacon*."

"I would be delighted, Miss Dorie. Angela is openin' up about now. I could sure use the caffeine." Riley opened the squad car door for her and shut it after she was settled.

***

After driving up to Ross's house on the mountain outside Helen, GA, Dorie tried to sleep during the available two hours, but she kept tossing and turning thinking about the records office. *Twins? Babies switched at birth? Who have similar names and traits?* Finally, she threw back the covers. *Who would know? The hospital? And Mrs. McDonough.*

Could Riley and his mom be in danger?

After a quick shower, she drank her cup of coffee while her fawn and white greyhound Lilith Rising Star, Star for short, ran the backyard in the cool late September morning. After securing Star in the house, Dorie headed back down to Daelin to the *Beacon*. She submitted her current article then started working on the registrar burglary. *There must be a story in that.*

"Anyone seen the crime blotter during the last week or so?" She called out over the busy newsroom.

Alexander waved his hand in the air as he typed. Dorie hurried over to his desk.

"What's new there?"

Alexander handed her a page of handwritten notes. "Just promise you won't scoop me, new girl. I noticed an increase in break-ins including the one you worked last night with the Captain." He looked up and jabbed a sharp pencil through the last entry. "I mean, seriously, who would want to burgle a dusty place that keeps all its records on index cards? Surely it would be easier to hack the records online."

"Well, that's sorta what I'd like to know. Any similar break-ins?"

Alexander leaned back from the keyboard. "No, but they're weird. The hospital, the registrar, the local community college, Captain McDonough's house, and Mrs. McDonough's home."

"Curiouser and curiouser. What's the angle on your story?" Dorie chewed the pencil she carried.

"Just that we are no longer an innocent small town. We need to begin locking our doors with people coming into our community to break-in. No reason to let it be easy for 'em." Alexander leaned back in the chair. "What's your angle, Dorie?"

"Not sure yet. I need to ask some more questions before I know if I have something. Write your piece. Some folks will be appalled. Can I make a copy of your notes?"

"You can have it. I'm done with it."

Dorie snatched a soft peppermint from his candy jar, walked back to her desk, and began typing.

"Burglary at the Records Office. First clue, broken glass with blood. Second clue, only one drawer disturbed. This reporter rode along with Captain McDonough and was first on the scene with him. Despite the mess, only two cards were taken, as far as can be determined.

"Ten unsolved cases sit on the police blotter today. How many more before the police can identify the culprit and determine the motive? Anything missing from your house, car, garage? Send a tip to Dorie Hudson, *The Daelin Beacon*."

Chapter 3
Checking in …

L ooks good."

Dorie startled and looked up to see the editor, her boss, Mr. Andrews looking over her shoulder.

"Imagine. A crime spree in Daelin." Mr. Andrews took the seat beside her desk. "Lilah wanted me to ask if you'd like to stay in our mother-in-law cottage when you're working in town, so you won't need to drive to Helen every night."

"Now that would be great, except I have a dog at home. Emmie lets her out at midmorning and on her way home, but I don't want her alone all night."

"Well, I think that's half the reason Lilah wants you to stay over." Mr. Andrew scratched his head. "She's thinking about getting a support dog to help her."

Dorie nodded. "That would be a good thing, but Star isn't trained for that."

"We could try it for a week and see how it goes, if you like."

"Sounds great. I'll put together a suitcase tonight and bring Star to work with me tomorrow."

Mr. Andrews returned to his office while Dorie made appointments to visit those who had been robbed. She grabbed her computer bag and headed out to see Mrs. McDonough.

Dorie rapped on the McDonough front door. She could hear rustling in the house and heard the back-door slam. A figure climbed into an electric purple sports car and drove through the yard to avoid hitting her blue compact car. When he shifted into Drive, she caught a glimpse of him. Before she could raise her hand in recognition of Riley, the car jumped into motion.

So that's odd. First, I didn't know Riley had a purple car. Second, he normally would wave. And third, why would he leave when I came to visit his mother?

Mrs. McDonough opened the front door to her and hugged her, a little too tightly. "My dear Dorie. Riley's been so worried about you being alone out in Helen by yourself. Let's go in for sweet tea."

Sweet tea is about a cup or more of sugar for a gallon of tea, steeped in the sun, and served over ice. Dorie watched Mrs. McDonough mix it up and pour it into the tall glasses. The sugar crystals glistened as they escaped the pitcher. She also opened a store-bought package of cookies but arranged them on a crystal tray. After all, this was the South.

"Are you okay?" Dorie noticed Mrs. McDonough's hand seemed to quiver as she drank her tea. "Was that Riley who just left here in such a hurry?"

"Please call me Mama Mary. Most people do." She took another sip of sweet tea. "No, no, he wasn't my Riley. He's a cousin to Riley. He was looking for some family tree information. Unfortunately, I didn't give him what he needed."

"But he nearly ran over my car and drove in your yard. Forgive me, but that seems a little more than disappointed." Dorie ran her finger on the edge of the sugar-encrusted rim of her glass. "I know I already asked this, but are you okay? You seem shaky."

Mama Mary looked up from her tea and took a deep breath. The pause offered Dorie the sense that Mama Mary was searching for a way to tell the story without overtly lying.

What is this all about? Dorie took an iced sugar cookie to give Riley's mom a chance to gather her thoughts. As she chewed, she watched Mama Mary shred the paper napkin into bits. *All was not well here.*

Dorie reached across the table and took Mama Mary's hand. "You don't have to tell me anything else about that. Can you tell me about the break-in here a week or so ago?"

Mama Mary's face relaxed. "Oh, yes. I was at choir practice when it happened. I was startled to find my back door open after I put the car in the garage out back. When I went in, the house was a mess, as though a twister had gone through it. Papers were everywhere. Books were pulled off the shelves. Of course, I called the police."

"That must have been frightening. Was anything taken?" Dorie took a sip of tea. She could feel her blood sugar rising.

"That was the odd thing. Whoever it was took our family Bible and photo albums. Of all the things I have, those are the only ones that can't be replaced." Mama Mary used what was left of her napkin to dab at the tears that had begun. "Riley's baby album too."

"Surely you have ways to reprint the pictures. You should have negatives. I bet Greg at the *Beacon* could help with that." Dorie scooted her chair closer so she could wrap her arm around Riley's mother. "Do you have the negatives?"

"There's a box with all the negatives from vacations, theme parks, and people in the top of the closet. It would take forever to squint at those film strips to find the right ones to print."

"We have a light table in the back room of the *Beacon.* I can lay out bunches of them to see which ones should be printed. Let me do this for you. It's the least I can do after Riley helped save me from death." Dorie got up. "Which closet?"

If the box of negatives had been any larger, it would not have fit in the back of Dorie's compact car. She had no desire to haul it up the mountain either, so she stopped by the *Beacon* and shoved the box in the back room next to the old light table.

While leaving, she realized she'd forgot to ask Mama Mary about the other birth record.

Chapter 4

Spending the night …

Like most mornings, when Dorie opened the curtains, she saw clouds, not in the sky, mind you, but right outside the window. The sun wouldn't burn the condensation away for another hour or so. Some days, the house would be in the clouds the majority of the day. It was actually one of the things Dorie enjoyed about Ross's house above Helen, GA. It reminded her of playing princess as a young girl. Her private tower in the clouds. It was only when she was a teenager that she learned about Britain's Tower and its dark history. She was safe here in her castle in the clouds.

Dorie packed the car with Star essentials, including her crate, while her greyhound ran laps around the yard. She needed a second crate for this house sharing plan to work out. Her luggage included about one week of Dorie's work essentials. On the weekends, she would return for Star's sake, as well as her own peace of mind.

She stepped inside the gate with Star's collar and

leash. "Come on, Star. We're going for a ride."

Star bolted across the yard but stopped just before plowing over her 'mommy'. Dorie slipped the martingale collar over her nose after several false attempts due to an open, smiling mouth. Finally, she buckled Star into her safety vest and tethered her in the back seat. The last thing she needed while driving down the mountain was a greyhound in the front seat. Truth be told, she needed a bigger car if she was going to be taking Star anywhere often. And the back of Ross's pickup was not appropriate for a nervous sight hound.

Lilah Andrews met Dorie and Star at the door in her wheelchair. "I'm so excited that you accepted our invitation." Lilah reached out to the dog and stroked her head. "I just know you and I are going to be good friends, Star."

"You must be careful about the doors to outside. An open door is an invitation to run like the wind like she did at the track." Dorie came in, closed the door, and unclipped Star's leash. She handed it to Lilah. "Put it on her before you open the front door. Tell her to wait."

"I don't normally have company. It's a quiet block. She can lay beside me while I knit, embroider, and read." Lilah took Star's head and rubbed it. "I look forward to seeing if I can keep up with her."

Dorie set up the crate in the Andrews' home while planning to buy a second one for the cottage. "Don't let her pull you over. She's strong but gentle. Tell her what you want from her. She's smart. She'll understand."

"Thank you for trusting me with Star. So much is being taken away from me with MS. I'm excited to have something good added."

Star trotted over to the folded-up plaid blanket between the recliners and lay down.

"Glad to help. She makes me smile too." She gave her other helpful dog-sitting instructions for a novice greyhound minder. "I better get going. My boss will be annoyed if I'm much later."

Lilah waved her hand. "Ethan would want you to get settled in the cottage before you go in. Take your time."

When Dorie arrived at the offices of the *Beacon*, the newsroom was already empty with the staff in the conference room. "Good morning, I'm late because I was setting up an experiment."

Mr. Andrews nodded, and the rest of the staff looked down at their notes. Dorie took her acquired normal seat and got out her tablet to take notes.

"Good of you to join us. I repeat. We need to know who this burglar is before he or one of our citizens is hurt. Find the common denominator, folks." Mr. Andrews smoothed his beard and looked intently into each reporter's face. "Maybe we can solve this faster than the police. That's it for today. Hudson, my office."

That's where Dorie went as the crowd dissipated. As she waited for her boss to come, her phone vibrated in her pocket. Six AM on the West Coast. Ross. She popped up the FaceTime call.

"Hello, Beautiful!" Ross was bare-chested, sitting on the side of his bed.

"How are things on the coast?" Dorie didn't use a term of endearment because she hadn't had time to settle on one before he moved, temporarily, to California the first of September. "Plant many trees?"

"Bunches. Did you move to the Andrews' guest house today like you were talking about?" Ross moved to the kitchenette in his hotel room and started a cup of coffee. "What's the latest on those burglaries?"

Dorie checked to see if Mr. Andrews was coming yet. "Not sure, somehow Riley is the focus. I don't know what's going on."

"You'll figure it out, News Lady. I miss you. We have so much we need to decide and more time to spend together." Ross sipped his K-cup coffee. "And I am so anxious to get back to my fancy coffee machine."

Dorie smiled. "I'm sure I'll miss it by the end of the week, too. When do you think you'll be able to come back for a visit?"

"For sure Thanksgiving week in St. Louis, but I'd like to be back sooner. I miss you more than I miss the coffee machine."

Dorie laughed. "So now I rate more than coffee? When did that happen?"

Ross walked out onto the balcony of his hotel room showing her the ocean in the distance. "This view cannot hold a candle to being in Helen with you."

"I love you too. I gotta go. I'm in Andrews's office, and he's on his way."

"Love you, Dorie. I'm only here to make a better

future for us both. Have a great day." He threw her a digital kiss and rang off.

Dorie had tears in her eyes as she clicked her phone off and looked up to see Mr. Andrews across the desk from her. She knew from the heat traveling up her neck that he'd been there longer than she'd realized. She stashed her phone in her bag. "What can I do for you?"

"I have no problem with you using my office for those very important phone calls from Ross. That's one reason I told you to come in here. Privacy is a valuable commodity, especially in a newsroom." He sat down behind the cluttered desk. "Greg tells me you brought a big box of negatives here from Mary McDonough. What's that about?"

"Two things, actually. The thief took photo albums, Riley's baby book, and the family Bible. First, I offered to replace important photos for her. Second, I thought it would give me an idea of what the thief was after."

"That's pretty brilliant. Greg's at your disposal. Good work." As Dorie stood to go, he added, "Glad to have you staying with us and allowing Lilah to care for Star. It will give her purpose when I'm not there."

Dorie nodded. "Glad I can help." Then she headed to the back room to the light table and the box of negatives. She opened the box and sighed. *What have I gotten myself into? What's so important in this box to warrant all these break-ins?*

Chapter 5
Lighting the past …

Dorie stood and rubbed the back of her neck. She'd bent over the light table all morning. So many zoo pictures. So many vacations to Stone Mountain, Six Flags Over Georgia, Braves' games, and World of Coke. Several things were apparent: Riley's dad was not in the picture, literally and figuratively. Mama Mary worked hard to give Riley everything she possibly could. Ross was in many of the pictures, and the three of them were inseparable.

"Here's the first batch of photos you asked for." Greg startled her with his entrance. "Pretty fun working with film again. I'm digitizing these so you can print whatever you need. Everything is digital these days. Lucky Mama Mary kept these. Most of everyone's memories are toast if the cloud crashes." He handed her the prints she'd identified as significant.

"Thank you. I know this is grunt work, but maybe a clue will arise." Dorie picked up another stack of film strips. "Can you print these too?"

"Sure thing, Dorie." Greg headed back to his scanner and photo paper.

She had barely made a dent in the stack of negatives by lunch even though she'd weeded out many strips as extraneous. She sorted negatives into vacation, people, and unnecessary. Sunsets, sunrises, and ocean are great but not relevant to her investigation. However, before she chucked anything, she labeled the strip and recorded it on her tablet. She also set aside a few strips of little boy Ross.

Time for lunch. Not only was being hunched over the light table exhausting, but it was hot. *LEDs would cool this thing down.* Dorie opened the lightbox and took a picture of the light sources inside.

After lunch and a trip to the hardware store for cool LED bulbs, Dorie decided to check out the other burglaries. She headed to the DMV to get info on the purple car. Her press credentials helped her bypass the busy line. She waited a few minutes until the director asked her into his office.

"How can I help, Miss Hudson?" The man sat down and booted his computer.

"An electric purple sports car has been identified near recent burglaries."

The director brought up the database on cars in Georgia. "Could it be a Mustang?

"That could be it." Dorie perched on the edge of her chair wishing she could see what was on the screen.

"Looks like it was stolen Friday night while the owner, a Dr. Eminem, was changing to go out on the town with his girl. Then he saw it, driving away. Can't imagine he was too happy. End of story so far."

"Where was this?" Dorie took notes on her phone.

"Looks like the Athens campus area. Why? Do you know where it is or who has it?"

Dorie shook her head. "Not yet. I'm working on it though. The Daelin police are working a string of cases involving that car." She handed him her business card. "Can you call me if you find out more?"

He took her card but gave her a grim look. "By the time the DMV is involved, it's pretty much over."

Dorie headed back to the Andrews' to take Star off their hands. She knocked on the storm door, and Star greeted her on the other side. Mr. Andrews held Star back while Dorie handled the door. When she saw the crate, Dorie smacked her forehead.

"I forgot to get another crate for the cottage." Dorie plopped into a recliner. "I need to go back out, so we don't have to dismantle the setup in here."

"No, you don't." Lilah wheeled her wheelchair over to her and patted her knee. "Ethan went by the pet store and bought the exact same setup as what you brought here this morning. It's all ready for our girl to have a good rest with her mommy in the cottage."

"Wow. I don't know what to say. Thank you." Suddenly Dorie could tell it would be an early night. "Then I'd best take Star to her home away from home and get dinner."

Just then the doorbell rang.

"Pizza's here. We ordered enough for you too."

It was growing dusky as Star and Dorie headed

out-back to the cottage. Sure enough, the crate was ready for Star who went straight in, turned around, and flopped. Dorie left the door open in case she wanted to snuggle later.

While Star snored, Dorie unpacked her things and made herself a K-cup of coffee. Just as the final jet of steam and water finished the brew, she heard Ross 'drop in' on her Alexa Show she'd brought with her from Helen. Dorie had insisted that they invest in the newest communication technology since he'd be gone for six months. It reminded her that she should get her mom one for Christmas.

"Are you in, Dorie?"

Dorie hurried to the living space in the cottage with her cup. "I'm here."

"You look tired, News Lady. Tough day?" He was in his National Parks uniform and covered in dirt.

"You look like the trees won today." Dorie took a sip. "Going out after you clean up?"

"Nah. I brought back a sub sandwich and chips. I know. Not the best, but I'm tired." Ross took a bite and sipped his coffee. "What are you working on?"

Dorie filled him in with the developments on the case.

"Hey, one of the professors in Athens had an electric purple Mustang when I was there during college. Dr. Eminem was an engineering instructor. Students called him Dr. Enigma because he was a puzzle to everyone. He had another nickname, but that wouldn't be helpful." Ross ate some more of his sandwich.

"I can imagine. Do you think I should drive to Athens to talk to him?"

"Couldn't hurt. It's not too far from you." Ross emptied his chips, crunched up the bag, and shot it at the trash can. "Missed."

"I should go to bed, Ross. I'll be back at the light box in the morning. Maybe I will go on to Athens and ask Dr. Enigma questions about his car."

"Don't forget I love you. Six months will fly by. You'll see." Ross threw a digital kiss.

Dorie returned it and said, "Alexa, drop out."

She knew these six months without him were accomplishing his goal to work in the Chattahoochee Forest. She understood chasing dreams. That's how she ended up in Daelin, after all. Dorie wished she hadn't fallen for Ross right before he left. She twisted the diamond ring he'd given her. *Perhaps I should be using the time to plan a wedding. Doing it without him just seems wrong though.*

A sound outside her window roused Star who began to growl. Dorie closed her crate, so she wouldn't run out after someone and get lost, or worse, hurt.

Dorie opened the door to the cottage and looked out. A shadowy figure ran down the driveway from the cottage to the purple Mustang. *It's like he wants to be seen. And whoever he is looks a lot like Riley.*

Chapter 6

Discovering a peeping tom …

Dorie called Riley. "Purple car alert with guy at Andrews' cottage."

"What?" His voice sounded foggy. "Say that again."

"Riley, our suspect was looking in the windows at Andrews' cottage then drove away in the purple car." Dorie tried not to sound exasperated, but she was. She'd figuratively been tracing the mystery man's steps since her call on Mama Mary. Now he was peeping in on her. No! She wouldn't have it. "Maybe he left fingerprints on my window ledge."

"Good thought. I'll send forensics by." He cleared his throat and coughed. "Dorie, were you hurt?"

"Terrified, perhaps." *What was wrong with this man?*

"Take Star and go into the Andrews' house. Whoever this is targets my closest friends and family. I'll not let him take you too. Ross charged me with caring for you after all."

"What's happened?" Dorie was becoming

concerned. "Has someone been hurt?"

"Yes. My dog was poisoned in my own backyard. Animal cruelty may not reach the level of murder, but in this case, it should." He sounded broken. "Don't take any chances, Dorie. Go now either into Andrews' house or drive up the mountain. Don't be a sitting duck."

Riley hung up before Dorie could respond. The knock on the door startled her. She opened Star's crate and put her collar and leash on. Then she went to the door, with her greyhound pulling her. When Dorie opened the door, her visitor was Ethan Andrews.

"Everything okay?"

Dorie filled him in while they waited for the forensics van to arrive. After answering the technicians' questions, Dorie went in her pjs to her boss's house and tried to sleep in one of their guest beds. Star finally settled down in her crate from home while the crime scene guys looked for some sign that the mystery man had been there.

Dorie's phone woke her from a nightmare as sunlight streamed through the windows. She picked up the phone to find Ross's face.

"Hey, Sweetheart! You're not up yet? What's happened?"

Dorie jumped up from the bed and looked at the clock. "Holy cow, it's already nine."

"That's when I normally call. I repeat, what's happened?"

Dorie told him about the presence of the guy with the purple car at the guest house.

"You don't sound safe. What can I do?"

Dorie sighed. "From there, about all you can do is pray. I gotta go, Ross." She jabbed the red button, let Star out of her crate, and released her into the fenced backyard.

"Ethan said to let you sleep. I gather we had unexpected company last night." Lilah rolled her chair over to Dorie's side and took her hand. "They'll catch this guy soon. Just stay safe in the meantime."

Dorie left Star with Lilah then went back to the cottage, dressed, and gathered her things for the day.

When she arrived at the *Beacon*, Riley was there with his police car.

"Are you all right, Dorie?" He gave her a hug, one she great appreciated.

"I'm annoyed that this guy is running around terrorizing Daelin. You need to catch him." Dorie stabbed a finger into his chest. "Ross thinks I should bow out of the investigation."

"He could be right. I'd never forgive myself if something happened to you on my watch." He bent and kissed her.

Dorie jumped away like she'd been shot. "I'm engaged to Ross," she whispered.

"I know, I'm sorry, forgive me." Riley put his hands in his pockets. "I better get back at it. Let me know if you find out anything."

Dorie nodded. How could she tell Ross that his best friend had just kissed his fiancée? Did that fall under 'need to know' and perhaps he didn't need to know? After all, it was only one kiss, initiated by him.

She watched Riley drive away then turned into the

office. No one said a word about her lateness nor if they'd seen the kiss. Mr. Andrews must have explained the situation about being late. No explanation about the kiss would help anything.

Greg had piled new prints on the light box from the negatives she'd given him. Nothing new in these pictures. More of Mama Mary with Riley. Because Dorie was going through the box last one in first one out, the pictures of Riley showed him growing younger the deeper she got in the box. She organized the prints younger to older. *Who's that?* Someone in the crowd for Riley's police academy graduation caught her eye. She grabbed the magnifying glass beside the light box. The man with the purple car! At Riley's graduation. And looking for all the world like Riley himself.

Cousin? Possible but exceedingly difficult. Twin? Surely Mama Mary would have raised them both. At the very least, she would acknowledge his existence. An older brother? If so, why would he not have been part of Riley's life? That picture brought up more questions than answers. At least it confirmed the reason she'd thought he was Riley. In a Bond movie, the antagonist would have had plastic surgery to look like someone else so he could take over the person's life for a time. However, this was no movie, and it would be ridiculous. What would someone hope to accomplish playing Riley McDonough?

When her phone rang, Dorie startled and dropped the magnifying glass. It shattered on the concrete floor of the storage room. Dorie answered to see Ross's face again.

"Good morning, News Lady. I know it's not my

usual time…" Ross squinted into his phone. "Are you okay?"

"The phone startled me is all." Dorie leaned the phone in the crook of her laptop. "Guess I'm still a little stressed from last night."

"Why don't you take some time off and come visit me? We could make it a long weekend."

"I can't take off now. I need to help Riley with this case." Dorie folded her arms.

"Shouldn't the police be doing that?"

"Of course, they are, but I'm helping. Just like we did with Trudy's case." Dorie already wished this conversation finished.

"And you were nearly killed, Dorie. Perhaps you should keep a lower profile."

"I need to go, Ross. I still have work to do for the *Beacon*. I love you, but I've got to go." Dorie stabbed the red Facetime button. *If he really wanted to help, he could come back and be here with me.*

***

Ross looked at the blank screen on his phone. It wasn't like her to hang up on him. And this was the second time today. What was going on?

"Ok, Ross?" The foreman on his crew came over to him. "Problems with your girl?"

"'Course not. It's just the long-distance thing. Hard to keep the subtexts clear." Ross pocketed his phone and leaned against a stump. "I'm sure it will be fine."

But Ross was finding it hard to let it go. It was harder than he'd thought to be away from Dorie and Daelin.

***

Dorie swept up the broken glass, then she worked her way through the box until noon when she felt she could barely see anymore. Time for lunch and a road trip. She drove through Chick-Fil-A for nuggets, fries, and a Cherry Coke. She entered the address for the University of Georgia into her GPS. Ross's alma mater. *Could I find out more about Ross from before his grandpa's death?*

Chapter 7

Experiencing a flashback …

The University of Georgia, the home of the Bulldogs, Ross's alma mater. As Dorie drove onto campus, memories of her days at Virginia Tech came flooding in on her, triggering both happy and sad feelings. What no one knew in Daelin was that she had been engaged before to another journalism student, Elliott Nelson. Elliott had saved her life their senior year and lost his at the same time to a campus shooter. If he hadn't stepped between the shooter and her, she probably would have died. He had lingered over several weeks, but ultimately Elliott had sacrificed himself for her. *Greater love has no man than this: that he lay down his life for his friends. John 15:13 (NIV)*

Dorie wiped tears that blurred her vision in order to read and follow the signs to the engineering building. When she pulled into the parking spot, emotion overwhelmed her. She wept bitter tears.

Father God, how could I have put what happened a year ago aside so easily? How could I be wearing another man's ring so soon? How could I have forgotten so much given to me?

As Dorie prayed, a tapping came at her car window. She rolled it down while frantic to wipe away her tears.

"Ma'am, are you all right?" The man had a Middle Eastern accent and was tall, dark, and thin. "Are you hurt? Can I help?" He handed her his cloth handkerchief.

"It's a soul hurt, sir. I'm actually here to see Dr. Eminem." She wiped her tears.

"Then you have found him. Come, I have tea in my office. Good for the soul hurt."

Dorie rolled up the window and turned off the car. She stepped out of the car, then grabbed her backpack from the backseat.

"Ah, Miss Dorie Hudson, I have been expecting you. Let me take the bag for you."

Dorie allowed him to take it. "How do you know who I am?"

"Powers of deduction, like Sherlock Holmes." He turned the strap so she could see the embossed name on it. "Unlikely I would have two Dories see me in the same day, don't you think? This is about my car, yes?"

Dorie nodded. She saw how he might get the nickname "Dr. Enigma". He was mysterious, but wise and kind. When they arrived at his office, he started an electric kettle for tea.

"You said on the phone that your fiancé knew me. Who remembers me?" He moved a pile of books off a chair for her, then after she had settled, he handed her the backpack.

Dorie twisted the engagement ring on her left

hand. "Ross MacAvoy."

Dr. Eminem raised his hands in the air. "A wonderful man and gifted student. He could have studied any kind of engineering and been a success. He wanted to work in the National Forest, though."

She felt that if she spoke, she might break down in tears again.

He handed her a cup of hot water and a tea bag. "Sorry, I only have a sachet packet, or tea bags you might say. At home, I have many varieties of loose tea. So much better than this. Sugar? Cream?"

"No, this is fine, sir." Dorie set the cup aside to steep and pulled out her recorder and tablet. "Your purple car is driving around in Daelin, Doctor. The man driving it looks a lot like this." She showed him a picture of Riley.

"But surely this is Captain McDonough who was here this morning about the same matter. I'm sorry you have wasted a trip." Dr. Eminem sipped his tea. "I told him about a former student of mine. Ryker Johnson looks startling similar to your police chief. He was a student here until he was arrested for thievery. He spent two years in a detention center. Due to his record, the college would not readmit him this semester when he was released."

"So, Ryker stole your car, then?"

"After much wailing and gnashing of teeth about his college status, so it seems." Dr. Eminem sipped his tea. "I sent Captain McDonough to the registrar's office, but I doubt they will release the records you need without a warrant."

"But he stole your car." Dorie shook her head. "I don't understand."

"FERPA legislation keeps records private. I too don't understand. This man is a criminal. He gave up his rights."

Dorie and Dr. Eminem sipped tea in silence for a time while Dorie tried to figure out how to ask the other question on her mind.

"You had my fiancé Ross MacAvoy as a student here?" She hoped the question sounded innocent and smiled a sweet smile.

"Ross. He was a joy as a student. He was reserved even then, before his grandfather's death. I have talked to him several times in the five years since graduation." He took a sip. "However, he was not an avoider of pranks during his time here."

"Pranks?" Dorie could not imagine such a thing. "Are we talking about my Ross?"

Dr. Eminem finished his tea and nodded. "He was the one who gave me my nickname." He stood and picked up the nameplate on his desk. "Ross's doing, guaranteed. It's the quiet ones who need the most watching."

The nameplate he handed her read, "Dr. Enigma, a puzzle wrapped in mystery."

***

Dorie hurried to the registrar's office, hoping to catch Riley there. The police captain's SUV from Daelin was parked in a visitor's slot. She pulled in beside him and opened her door. As she stood up, a wave of nausea and recognition gripped her. Her heart raced and the perspiration began as the old flashback started.

It was at the registrar's at Virginia Tech that the shooter had come to settle a score with the dean of students. She could see the man as clear as though it was happening here and now. And Elliott was chasing him and shouting, "Not my Dorie! Shoot me instead!" Then he stepped in front of her as the bullet left the muzzle.

Dorie raced into the building to the restroom where she vomited her lunch and anything else the gag reflex could find. She'd dealt with this with counseling. She'd grieved his loss and suffered survivor's guilt. Why was this PTSD showing its ugly head now?

"Dorie? Is that you in there?" Riley's voice.

"I'm in here. I'll be right out." She wet paper towels to cleanse her face and try to still the desire to vomit again. She wiped away the tears, but her eyes were puffy. They'd give her away.

Dorie pushed open the door to find Riley in full captain's uniform and in severe concern mode.

"What happened? Did you eat something that disagreed with you? You're not pregnant, are you?" He grabbed an arm and steered her toward the busy cafeteria. "Let me get you a Coke."

Before Dorie could respond, he was gone to get her a drink. *Pregnant? Total impossibility.* She only knew one virgin who'd given birth.

When Riley returned with the sodas, Dorie nearly burst. "No, I could not be pregnant." All sound in the cafeteria stopped and eyes turned their direction. Dorie covered her face until sound resumed.

"Well, things happen." Riley handed her a Coke. "I'm not passing judgment, but you and Ross have spent a lot of alone time together, especially in Helen. So, what's wrong?"

"Short story? I was in a campus shooting. My fiancé stepped in front of me and took the bullet meant for me."

Riley scooted his chair closer and took her hand. "How would anyone know that? You never talk about yourself. Of course, Ross knows, right?"

"No. I had pretty much shoved it aside until I came onto this campus." Dorie had goosebumps running up her arms and uncontrolled shuddering. "How do I tell Ross?"

"Let me drive you home." Riley wrapped his arm around her

"And leave my car here? No." She pulled away.

Riley touched her arm. "Then let's go have an early dinner here in Athens before driving back. I can share what I was able to discover about Ryker Johnson."

Chapter 8

Telling Ross about Elliott …

Dorie followed Riley to Cheddar's Scratch Kitchen. The hostess sat them in a back booth, away from other late afternoon diners. They were silent as they perused the menu.

"Know what you want?"

The waitress startled her. Riley grabbed and held tight to her hand. He ordered and helped Dorie figure out something to eat.

As the waitress walked away, Dorie took her hand back. "Tell me about Ryker Johnson."

"Ryker Johnson. Born on the same day as me. Raised in the foster care system. Been in and out of trouble, including a juvie record and a two-year stint in prison." Riley unwrapped his silverware and stabbed the lemon with a fork several times before squeezing juice into his ice water. "I know what you're thinking, but I don't think Mama would have given up a child, especially into foster care."

"I guess I'm surprised he didn't come shoot up the Admin Building. That's what the guy did at Virginia Tech when he didn't get in." Dorie shivered though the air conditioning was not cold. "Elliott was the only one killed. It didn't get much press, like his life didn't matter. I plunged into my senior year studies and grief counseling. I managed to 'make it go away.'"

The waitress arrived with salads and bread.

Riley touched her hand. "Ross needs to know this just like I need to know who this Ryker guy is. Let's pray over the food. Lord, bless the food to the nourishment of our bodies. Heal our wounds and hurts. Give us closure and peace about it all. In Jesus' name, Amen."

Dorie played with the salad more than she ate. When the main course arrived, she shoved it aside.

"They have cherry pie if you eat your chicken nuggets." Riley scrunched his eyebrows. "You do need to eat something. After all, you threw up your lunch."

"I need to go to Helen and find the box with my engagement ring and clippings about Elliott before Ross calls." Dorie hugged herself. "Stay and eat. I'll get something at home. "

"Wait just a minute." Riley flagged down the waitress. "We need boxes to take this with us and the check. And add a cherry pie to go."

"How did you know cherry pie is my favorite?"

"Daelin is a small town, and I'm best friends with your fiancé." Riley grinned and wiggled his eyebrows.

Dorie laughed at his funny expression. "You're a good friend."

"Watch out. I might have ulterior motives." Riley held her left hand and moved her engagement ring back and forth. "If Ross wasn't my best friend, I might act on those motives. You know, to make you my girl."

Dorie pulled her hand away. "I need to go."

The boxes arrived with two takeout bags, a cherry pie and the check.

Dorie grabbed for the ticket. "Let me get this. I have an expense account for meals on assignment."

"Nope. This is police business." Riley snatched it before Dorie could reach it. "Besides, I promised Ross I'd look out for you in his absence."

When they hit the road, Riley followed Dorie into Daelin. Dorie checked on Star who remained with Ethan and Lilah while she headed up the mountain to Helen.

Dorie arrived at Ross's house and took the steps to the attic from the garage. A switch on the wall provided light in the shadowy stillness. *It had to be here. Surely it was moved into the attic with other boxes I haven't unpacked.* She sorted through the stacks of things: furniture, a trunk with hand stitched quilts, photo albums, and scrapbooks.

Finally, she found what she was looking for, a small box labeled 'personal'. "Ah, here it is." She picked up the box and as many photo albums as she could carry and made her way back down the steps.

She dumped her finds on the counter because the bistro table was too small for these things. *We really need a decent table for the kitchen or a set for the dining room. A living room couch wouldn't hurt either.* She popped the tape on the box just as her phone started singing Ross's ringtone, "Morning Coffee Jazz."

She answered the Facetime call just as she spied

the blue velvet ring box inside the carton.

"Where are you? I tried dropping in on you, but you weren't at the cottage." Ross wore his worried face. "What's going on? Did you see Dr. Eminem? What about the purple car?"

Dorie shook her head. "Relax. I'm home, in Helen. I didn't stop and pick up the Show."

"Okay, what's happening?" His face was still contorted, but his voice had come down a bit.

"I went to Athens and talked with Dr. Enigma." Dorie propped the phone on the counter next to the box then dragged a chair over. "Riley was there already. The man we're looking for is named Ryker Johnson. But something else happened while I was there."

She snatched up the velvet box and opened it. Her heart jumped in her chest to see the ring again. The diamond was small and surrounded by white gold embellishments. A tear slid down her cheek.

"What is it?" Ross waited for Dorie to explain.

Dorie turned the velvet box to the screen. "Last year I was engaged to someone else. He was shot and killed on campus almost a year ago. I buried it emotionally during grief counseling. Today at UGA, it all came flooding back."

"Sounds like something I wish I'd known." Ross twisted his lip and frowned. "Who was he?"

"Elliott Nelson." She trembled and stuttered. "He...he saved my life by giving up his own that day."

Dorie proceeded to unpack the box of memories, sharing them with Ross on Facetime. Pictures, mementos, and other scraps of her relationship with

Elliott. After she shared all the items in the box, Dorie put them back in.

"You need a better box for these memories. Go to the store and find a pretty box to put them in. When we have shelves, we can put it on a shelf. He saved your life. We should honor him."

Dorie nodded and wiped her eyes. "I didn't keep this from you. I hid it from myself."

"Wish I was there to hug you and kiss away your tears, sweet Dorie." He smiled at her. "I've got to go now. Phone is running low on power. Don't forget, I love you." At that, the screen went black.

Dorie was drained emotionally. She put the chair back at the bistro table and stood frozen, staring at the counter. Finally, she pulled the cherry pie from the fridge. After zapping it in the microwave, Dorie carried the pie up to the bedroom. She kicked off her shoes then climbed in bed with her clothes on. After eating her pie robotically, she scrunched down in a ball under the covers, unbidden tears wetting her pillow, and fell into a fitful sleep.

Chapter 9

Thinking on Elliott…

It was still dark when Dorie woke in the bed in Helen. After checking her phone, 4:30, she crawled from the bed. *One thirty on the West Coast. Too early to call Ross. Too early for Java Joint. Not too early for coffee.* Dorie slipped on her shoes, gathered the pie dish, and headed downstairs.

After fixing that cup of coffee, Dorie went out onto the deck. She was greeted with a cacophony of tree frogs, crickets, and early bird tweets. She popped open her laptop and wrote a tribute to Elliott Nelson.

A Tribute to Elliott Nelson
by Dorie Hudson
In the fall of 2018, Elliott Nelson
saved my life by giving his.
Elliott was my great college
romance. We became engaged that
fall, hoping for a June wedding after
graduation. Elliott studied
engineering, but he was a
renaissance man, loving art, music,
and theatre. He read Russian
literature and spoke fluent French.

His mop of brown hair fell into his dark brown eyes. His smile was crooked but wide.

He loved me, no doubt about it, and he loved God. As Christians, we waited for our wedding night.

In October, a man with a gun came onto our campus. He was angry with the administration for reasons I never understood.

That day, I needed to turn in my intent to graduate form. Elliott waited in his car for our trip into Blacksburg for lunch.

As I approached the entry, the man with the gun ran up the sidewalk toward me.

"Get out of the way, girl." He waved the gun at me. "I'll shoot you if you don't get out of my way."

I froze. Terror filled every fiber of my being. The man pointed the gun at me and fired, point blank.

The next thing I knew, Elliott dashed between us. The bullet hit an alternative target. My Elliott.

Elliott fell to the ground between us, bleeding from the chest. He spent weeks in the hospital before succumbing to his injuries.

Elliott Nelson saved my life. They couldn't save his. He was my first great love. He saved my life, so I could love again.

I'll never love without a tribute to
Elliott Nelson.

After sending it on to Ethan Andrews, her editor,
she went in the house for clothes she hadn't slept in.

The phone startled her. Six A.M. Still really early
for the West Coast.

"Hello?"

"I got the feeling I should call. Are you okay?" It
was Ross.

"How did you know I needed you?" The tears
began running down Dorie's face.

"Ah, now, sweetheart. We're connected, you
know, even if we're not yet married. I love you. How
are you, Dorie?"

"Still shook up. I feel so alone."

"You'll be okay again. I'm sure it will take time."
The silence was lonely too.

Ross was the one who finally broke it. "Did Dr. E.
remember me?"

"Yeah, he was great. He told us who the man is
who stole his car." Dorie sat on the edge of the bed
then laid down. "He said you played a prank or two
in your day there, including the name plate for his
desk."

"Guess I'm found out."

Dorie wiped her face with her hand. "He didn't
seem to mind."

"Why are you crying, Dorie?"

"I wrote an article about Elliott this morning. I
sent it to Ethan. Do you want to read it?"

"Yeah. I'd like that. Since I'm up so early."

Dorie laughed because he'd found a way in. A way to make it better. "I love you."

"I know. Have a good day, my love."

Dorie hung up and washed her face again. It would be all right.

She headed back down the mountain to Daelin. The early October air held a chill, a harbinger of autumn. Soon the leaves would be turning colorful reds, yellows, and browns. She went to the Andrews' house to check on Star. Lilah responded to her tap on the door.

"It's not too early to visit my dog, is it?"

As soon as she spoke, the leggy greyhound rushed to her side, jumping and nuzzling. "Guess she's missed me."

"Of course, she missed you. She's a very intelligent dog. She knows who her mommy is."

Dorie came into the warm kitchen and sat down, so she could give her dog the love she hadn't been able to give her lately. Velvety soft fur, sloppy kisses, and long nose pokes into her warmed her heart. She wasn't alone, even if Ross was in California.

Then she went into the *Daelin Beacon*.

When Dorie arrived, Ethan was already in his office. She poked her head in. "I thought I was early."

"Come in. Tell me about Elliott and Ryker Johnson." He never looked up from his screen but motioned her into a chair. "How come I've never heard about Elliott before now?"

"PTSD." What else was there to say? She buried

the experience, so she could get through each day without crippling depression. "I loved him. He saved my life by giving his."

"Good piece. I'm running it next edition. Who is Ryker Johnson?"

"That's a good question. I haven't quite got it figured out, at least not proven yet."

"What's Riley got to say on it?" Ethan stretched back in his CEO desk chair.

Dorie tried to relax by scooting back into the chair. "He's flabbergasted. No idea what to think. It's very personal and emotional for him. Especially after someone poisoned his dog."

"What are you thinking?"

"I think Ryker is his brother. I don't know why, but Mama Mary only raised Riley. I've got a photo of Ryker at Riley's graduation from the Police Academy. Then he was in prison for a short stint. He was recently released. His release fits the timing of the burglaries and robberies, including the purple car theft."

"But it's only conjecture." Ethan came back to his desk. "Prove it. I think Riley's too close to the case. Do what you've got to do."

"Agreed." Dorie sighed and stood. "Guess I'm back at the lightbox this morning."

Ethan stood when she did. "By the way, did you see the news? California's on fire again. The Santa Ana winds are forecast to be near hurricane strength. Bad news for fire fighters and property owners." He stepped around the desk and perched on it in front of Dorie. "Any news from Ross?"

"I talked to him last night and this morning. He

didn't say much about it." Her intuition tingled. Ross was in trouble. But what could she do?

Dorie headed back to the negatives and the lightbox, then she sent Ross a text. "What is happening with the fires there? Are you safe?"

She tried to relax. He wouldn't see her text until it was his lunchtime.

After a couple hours of staring at the negatives, she felt bug-eyed. She was down to toddler years. Riley's grandparents were in the pictures now. But still no father. With just another inch of negatives to explore, Dorie needed coffee, sunlight, and looking at things at a distance. It was lunch at Java Joint time.

As Dorie stepped out of the offices of the *Beacon*, a firetruck flew by with sirens and horns blaring. Riley pulled up next to her in his chief's SUV. "Climb in! It's my mom's house."

Chapter 10

Burning down the house …

The house was fully engulfed when they arrived at the scene. Riley jumped out of the car and headed toward the house.

"Where's my mom? Where's my mom?" Shouting over the commotion involving the fire, he headed for the front door only to be restrained by the fire chief. Several others held him back as well.

"That's the man! That's the man I saw. He was wearing that uniform. He's the one who tried to kill Mama Mary." The neighbor was hysterical and pointing at Riley. "He was here, wearing his uniform. He drove away in a purple car."

Firefighters carried Mrs. McDonough out of the front door to a waiting stretcher. The porch fell in just afterwards as the blaze consumed the house. The people holding Riley back let go of him, and he sprinted to her side. Dorie joined him.

"Mama!" Riley had streams of tears rolling down his face. "Don't leave me, Mama!"

EMTs worked all around her, shoving Riley aside. Their hurried dialogue in medical jargon was not understood by Riley or Dorie. After hanging an IV of fluids, strapping on an oxygen mask, and cutting away burned clothing, the EMTs hurried the gurney toward the waiting ambulance. One paramedic stayed with Riley to explain.

"The good news is she's breathing on her own, and she doesn't appear to be burned." He paused as though gathering strength. "The bad news is she's unconscious and has been badly beaten. It's hard to know how much smoke inhalation has occurred."

"You mean someone beat her and set her house on fire? And the neighbor thinks it was me in a purple car?" Riley put his head in his hands. "Was it Ryker Johnson? Why would anyone do such a thing?"

"I don't know, Cap, but let's get her to the trauma center and help her come back to you. We may need to take her to Atlanta once she's assessed here." The medic headed toward the waiting ambulance. The siren began before he even pulled the doors closed.

"Purple car. I saw your look-alike driving Dr. Enigma's purple car the day I visited your mom." Dorie put her hand over her mouth. "She said he was your cousin, and he was mad that she didn't have what he wanted."

"I don't have any cousins that I know of. I don't know who Ryker Johnson is." Riley strode back to the car. "Hop in. Leave the fire officials to their work, and let's get going on ours." As he started the car, the roof fell into the house, and the fire burst through it.

Riley dropped Dorie off at her car in front of the *Beacon. Now those negatives are very important to this case. Who would want to hurt Mama Mary?*

Dorie decided to walk down Main Street to the Java Joint for lunch and some rumination.

As Dorie walked in, Angela called out to her. "Double shot mocha with a chicken salad croissant."

"You got it, Angie." Dorie made her way to 'her' booth in the back. She set up her laptop and joined the WI-FI. *Could I find this mysterious cousin online?* She googled McDonough and Ryker Johnson and looked at the possible choices. *Needle in a haystack.*

"Here ya go, Sweetie." Angela slid the plate and mug in front of her. "You look all kinda troubled. Is Ross giving you a problem?"

Dorie paid the tab. "No, it's not about Ross. It's Riley's mom and her home that just burned down. The neighbor just declared that Riley was seen, in uniform, leaving the house in a purple car."

"Well, that can't be right. Riley is way too conservative to drive anything purple." Angela sat across from her. "And I know he'd never hurt his mama."

"Know anything about a lookalike cousin named Ryker Johnson?"

Angela shook her head. "I'll let you know if I hear anything." She jumped up at the sound of the bell at the counter. "Keep your shirt on. I'm comin'."

Dorie texted Ross. "Riley's mom is in the hospital, and her home has been destroyed by arson."

Just then, Riley came by.

"Hey, sit here and tell me how things are."

The man showed no recognition of Dorie, but he slumped into the booth. The uniform was old, not Riley's new one with captain bars. This man also was unshaven and scarred. *This man is the lookalike. But how can I get the police here without suspicion?*

"How is your mom? I'm surprised to see you back so soon from the hospital." Dorie picked up her phone to read Ross's reply. Could she send a text without suspicion? "Just Ross. I had told him what had happened at your mom's house."

She swapped over to Riley's number and sent a quick text, "SOS, lookalike in uniform at my table at JJ." Then she turned the phone face down.

When he spoke, his voice was low and gravelly. "They wouldn't let me near her, so I left them to it. They may send her to Atlanta. Nothing I can do, so I came back here."

Angela swooped in with Riley's normal order, an espresso. "That's $3.50, as always. Can I get you anything else, Riley?"

The man handed her crumpled dollar bills and a handful of change. "Nah, I'm fine by this cup of joe."

Angela looked at him funny.

She knew! Don't tip him off! If only ESP was a real thing.

"Why don't you go ahead and take a sip, you know, in case it's not good enough." Angela crossed her arms, challenging the man.

He took a sip and spit it onto the floor. "There ain't no sugar in this cup. What are you playing at?"

"What are you playing at? Riley McDonough drinks that espresso with no sugar or cream day and night here. And this uniform looks like you slept in it, and then roughed up an old lady and set her house on fire. You may look like him, but that's as far as the resemblance goes."

The man jumped from his seat and shoved Angela

to the floor. Angela grabbed her arm in pain.

Dorie stood and glared at the man who pulled a very real gun from his holster. Sirens from just around the corner at the police station blared. He shoved Dorie back in her seat, then he backed out of the Java Joint through the alley exit.

Dorie jumped to Angela's side as police poured through the front door. At the gestures from patrons, they ran through to the alley. EMTs arrived on the scene and pronounced Angela's arm broken. They loaded her in the ambulance to take her to have it set and cast.

After they left with Angela, Dorie went back in and snagged the espresso cup holding it with a napkin. She poured the remaining coffee into her empty mug and waited for second-in-command Lt. Hank Curry to return and ask questions. Now those negatives seemed even more important. She was anxious to get back at the lightbox.

Chapter 11

Getting light on the situation …

Dorie was at the light box when Riley found her later that afternoon.

"I hear you and Angela met my lookalike. He broke her arm? What kind of a man shoves a woman to the floor with such force that she breaks her arm?"

Dorie switched off the light box. "He's not you." She wrapped an arm around his shoulders. "No one could think he was you in close proximity. How's your mom?"

"Still unconscious. They're running a concussion protocol. Has some smoke inhalation. The house is a total loss. Everything is gone." He shrugged her off. "I'm the police chief, but I can't even protect my mom or the barista at the coffee shop."

"I gave Hank the mug Angela served him. There should be prints."

Riley nodded. "Do you think he's my twin? Remember, you asked me that at the records office break-in. Why would Mama keep such a thing from me? And what are you doing with all these film strips?" He peered at one up to the light. "These are from my mom's house, aren't they?"

Dorie explained about the break-in and her initial desire to reproduce his baby book. "But later I began to think that the photos show something the burglar needed to know."

"Ironic, isn't it? You saved our old photos from the fire. The one thing everyone in a disaster misses most." Riley stood and stretched. "Do me a favor. Come by the station and help our sketch artist draw the lookalike with his scars and blemishes that make him look different from me."

"Will do." Dorie embraced him. "We'll get him. You look to arrest him. I'll work on these pictures and figure out why."

Riley hugged her back, then he kissed her. "I was quite serious about being attracted to you. If it was anyone but Ross ..." He leaned in for another kiss.

Dorie released him and stepped backwards. "Don't make this awkward. I really like you, but I love Ross."

"Message received. I'll let you get back at it." Riley ducked his head and left her. "I'll send the sketch artist to see Angela now."

She shook her head at his disappearing back. *Why did it have to be complicated?*

Dorie worked all afternoon on the negatives. Her eyes were itchy and blurry. Time to stop. Greg came in with more prints.

"You should give it a rest. You won't be able to see at all if you keep it up. Another bonus for the digital age."

"You're right. I better get back to the Andrews'

and relieve them of my big dog. I think I'll head up the mountain for the night."

Chapter 12

Burning California …

California statewide fire emergency" were the words that startled Dorie as her clock radio woke her. She jumped out of bed and ran down to the TV Ross had bought for them before he'd left for California. In brilliant color on the large flat screen, Dorie witnessed for herself the fires all over the northern and southern areas of California. Horror closed her throat.

"Ross." She ran over to the Alexa Show portal and gave the drop-in order. "Alexa, drop in on Ross."

The screen resolved showing his hotel room in the dark. They had agreed to avoid putting the video phone screen in their bedroom areas, so they would preserve some privacy before their wedding.

"Ross, are you there? Wake up! Wake up!" Tears streaked down her face. "Please be there. Sweetheart, please be safe."

Ross stumbled into the frame in his pajamas and ruffled hair. "Hey, Dorie. What time is it?"

"Have you seen the news? Turn it on. The state of California is on fire. Are you safe?" Dorie sat at the counter. "What will you do?"

Ross yawned while the hotel TV came on behind

him. "Dorie, I promise, I am okay. Everyone is aware of the danger. Some of the acreage I planted has burned. A waste of being away from you."

"What are you going to do? The fire is raging everywhere." Dorie clenched her fists and tried to regulate her breathing, but her heart hurt as it pounded in her chest. "I'm having a hard time living with you in California. How can I live if you die there?"

"No, no, no. Don't go there, News Lady. I am not going to die in California." Ross put his elbows on the counter and filled the screen with his face. "Try to relax. I'm flying out today. I'm coming home for a week or so, maybe till mid-November or so, until the fire crews have a handle on this emergency."

Her anxiety eased at this news. "You're coming home? When will I see you?"

"I have a flight out this morning, eventually into Atlanta. Can you come and get me?"

"I'd like nothing better. When do I need to be there?"

It was the last week in October.

Dorie had a few hours, so she went back to work at the lightbox. Just a few negative strips from the bottom of the box, she found something like what she was looking for. She jumped up from the lightbox to find Greg.

"Can you print this strip of pictures pronto? I'm headed to Atlanta in about an hour. I'd like to have them before I go."

Greg looked up from his computer screen. "You bet. It will be more exciting than what I'm doing.

What did you find?" He held the negatives up to the light. "Holy Smokes! I think you just found some answers. Ready in just a few."

Dorie pulled into Atlanta's Hartsfield-Jackson Airport, navigating the traffic and lanes leading to the pickup area. She'd been caught up in Atlanta traffic and was late. Ross was probably already out with his luggage. Then he came into sight, the gentle ginger-haired giant of a man in a National Parks uniform. Her man. Praise God he was safe and home.

She pulled her car over to the curb, threw it in Park, then jumped from the car to greet her fiancé properly. He dropped his bags to grab her up in his arms.

"I've been thinking about this moment all the way across the USA. It's even better than I imagined." Ross hugged her close before he kissed her soundly. "Let's head for the mountain, Sweetheart."

Ross deposited his bag in the back of the compact then wedged himself into the front seat. "You need a new car. I don't fit in this one."

"I know. Star doesn't either. I need a small SUV." Dorie focused on the lights and signs to find her way out of the complex maze of exit ramps. "We can look while you're home."

"How's Riley holding up with his imposter on the loose?" Ross leaned over and kissed her neck. "He must be going crazy."

"Worse. Ryker started hurting people Riley loves. And apparently poisoned his dog."

"That's low, killing a dog just as a vendetta."

"I'm so glad you are here where I can be sure you

are safe." Dorie's emotions had been on overload, ever since she'd woke to the emergency in California. "How long can you stay?"

"A couple weeks or so. Depends on the fires." Ross turned in his seat. "I'm beginning to think this whole Park Service thing is doing us more harm than good. You're shattered. I'm exhausted. We're too far apart to help one another. Should I quit?"

Dorie kept her eyes on the road though it became blurry with her tears. "I can't tell you to give up on your dream."

"I'd still have the opportunity in the Chattahoochee come spring. I just wouldn't have a job until then."

Dorie glanced at Ross. "Our needs are pretty frugal. No mortgage or rent. My car payment. Star's food. Food for us. Internet, phone, and TV. Gas to drive our vehicles."

"Yep. Should we go ahead and get married too? Y'know, since we'll be living in the same house?"

Dorie's heart clenched. That was faster than she'd expected. They'd planned it for next summer. Plenty of time, to make plans, to meet family, to know each other better.

"Should I be concerned that you're not answering right away, Dorie?" He placed a hand on her shoulder. "Have you already given up on us through this whole separation thing?"

"Of course not. Moving the wedding up doesn't give us any time to do the things we wanted to do, like meeting my family."

"I guess I don't think about stuff like that, having no family." He sounded wistful.

Dorie looked his direction. "Hey, I didn't mean anything about it. You never talk about your family."

"Nothing to say. They're gone. End of story."

Yet Dorie was sure there must be more to the story. He clearly had a mom and a dad at some point. What happened to them? He went silent for the rest of the drive to Emory Hospital.

She pulled into the parking lot. "I need to check on Mama Mary since we're in Atlanta. Want to come?"

"Yep, she was like a mom to me, too."

They hurried into the hospital and found her in ICU. Riley stood outside the room.

"How's she doing, buddy?" Ross pulled Riley into a bear hug. "I can't believe all you're going through."

Riley crumpled. "They don't think she's going to make it. Between the smoke inhalation and the broken bones from the beating, it may be more than she can overcome."

"Okay if I talk to her alone?" Dorie wanted answers before she showed the photos to Riley. "I might have a lead on our mystery man."

"That would be a good thing. He's driving me around the bend. Why does he hate me and Mama so much? It's like he's trying to destroy my life." Riley slumped into a chair in the hallway. "Go talk to her. I'm not sure she can tell you much with the oxygen mask on though. She's drifting in and out of consciousness."

She looked at Ross.

"Nah, I'll stay with Riley." He sat down beside him.

Dorie entered the ICU room. Machines whirred

and beeped, a ridiculous cacophony holding Mama Mary between death and life. Dorie sat in the chair beside the bed. Monitors of all kinds measured and monitored her injuries. The lights were dimmed but necessarily left on.

"Mama Mary, it's Dorie. We talked about your burglary. Remember I took a big box of negatives to the *Beacon* to try to salvage your family photos and perhaps find your attacker."

Mama Mary turned her head toward Dorie and mumbled.

"I have some photos to show you. Can you open your eyes and tell me what I'm seeing?"

Mama Mary opened her eyes with great effort. She struggled to turn toward Dorie.

"It's okay. I'll bring them to you." Dorie stood and held out a photo. "Can you tell me about this photo?"

"My twins." Her voice was croaky and filled with emotion. "Pa said Ryker died. I didn't know." Tears welled up in her eyes and spilled over her cheeks. "I could have raised both. Pa didn't think I could."

Dorie put her hand on her arm. "It's okay. You didn't know. So, Ryker is mad?"

Mama Mary nodded. "Thinks I played favorites. I didn't know."

One of the machines went wild, and nurses appeared from nowhere. One shooed Dorie from the room.

"What's happening?" Riley grabbed Dorie's arms. "What did she say?"

Dorie handed him the photo of a younger Mama Mary with two small baby boys. "She said her father told her Ryker had died. Apparently, he released him into the foster system instead."

"Seriously? What else did she say?"

"She said Ryker is angry that she played favorites, keeping you and not him."

Riley released Dorie. "He's my brother, and he's exacting a cruel revenge?"

Dorie shrugged. What else could she say?

The flurry of activity continued at Mama Mary's bed, until it stopped. Riley paced by the door, waiting for some news, some information about his mom. Finally, the doctor came out of the room.

"Captain McDonough, I'm sorry to tell you that your mother has passed. We did everything humanly possible. She's in the hands of her Lord Jesus."

Riley stumbled backwards as though he'd been punched in the gut. "How could he do this, no matter what he thought? She was his mother too. We need to find him. I need to talk to him, to explain, to perhaps find a way to forgive." He backed into the wall and slid down it into a crouched position.

Ross went to him, crouched, and laid hands on his shoulders. Then Ross prayed with him and for him. He also prayed for Ryker, the long-lost child who wanted to belong somewhere. When Ross finished, he pulled Riley to his feet. Tears stained Riley's face as well as Ross's. They hugged.

"I don't know why you're here, Ross, but I am grateful for it." Riley stuck his hands in the pockets of his jeans. "Thank you, Dorie, for uncovering the key to this mystery. Now we need to find him and bring him in from the dark." He embraced Dorie under the watchful eye of her fiancé.

"Whatever I can do, let me help." Ross clapped

him on the back. "I'm here until the wildfires die down in California." Ross pulled Dorie closer to him and away from Riley.

Riley pulled a handkerchief from his back pocket and wiped his face. After a cleansing sigh, he turned to them. "Go on home. I'm sure I need to deal with paperwork before I can leave. I'll catch up with you later." Riley turned and entered the ICU room alone.

Chapter 13

Making plans for the future …

As they escaped Atlanta proper, the traffic eased up.

"What are you thinking?" Dorie kept her eyes on the road while she waited for his reply. "You're so quiet, even for you."

Ross took in a deep breath and sighed. "Like I said before, Mama Mary was like my mom too. She fed me snacks and dinner, sometimes. I stayed the night at that house more often than I can count. I knew all the nooks and crevices in that house for hide and seek. We were like brothers."

He fell silent. Dorie knew he'd share more if she stayed quiet. She glanced toward him.

"He's driving Dr. Enigma's car? Funny that connects to me instead of Riley." He stoked the red stubble on his face. "You found me in some of those photos, right?"

"Lots of them. I can tell you were close." *But what happened to your mom?*

"Yes. They were my family besides my grandparents." Ross wiped a tear from his cheek. "So, you and Riley seem pretty close."

Awkward silence ensued. Dorie didn't want to

cause any problems between Riley and Ross. What could she say that was the truth? Riley had been flirting, for sure. She'd never let it get more than that though.

"We've been working together to solve this mystery." Dorie had no desire to share the romantic vibes Riley had been sending her. "He's a good man, and he's been here."

She flipped on her blinker to exit the highway and head for Helen.

"And I haven't been, is that what you're saying?" Ross's voice caught in this throat. "Is there something I need to know about you and Riley, Dorie?"

"No. Nothing is going on. I love you, Ross." Those darn tears again. "You have nothing to worry about. I love you."

He took her hand. "And I love you."

They drove up the mountain to home.

Star bounded to the door as Ross entered. She jumped up but controlled her bounce.

"Bet you'd like to go out for a run, huh, girl?" Ross rubbed her neck and thumped her sides. "Come on, I'll let you out."

Dorie called out to Ross. "You know, 'cause I never let her out or play with her."

The back door slammed followed by the sound of a running greyhound. Dorie walked out onto the deck and watched Ross encourage Star to run full out. She sat down on the chaise lounge, almost sitting on a photo album. *Why was that out here?* Dorie would never have left a photo album outside, even if it was screened. Besides she'd not had a chance to even look at them.

Someone had been here and looked through this album. The hair on her neck stood up. *Who would it have been?* Dorie picked up the album and opened it. Baby Ross and a young woman were at the start. The rest of the pages had Ross with his grandparents, and only a young Ross with his grandfather. *What had happened to this family in this place?*

Soon Star and Ross bounded onto the deck. Star immediately found her outdoor bed and curled up in it. Ross flopped down on the other chaise.

"You get that album from the attic?" He panted from playing with the dog.

"Yes, the night I got the box of Elliott memoirs down. But I didn't leave it out on the deck. I think someone has been here." Dorie shivered. Even though the breeze was chilly, it wasn't the breeze that chilled her.

Ross reached across to her. "Now, your mind is working overtime on Riley's mystery. It's okay. I'm here now." He pulled the lounge chair next to hers and cuddled her close.

"I guess that's possible. Is this your mom?" She showed him the first page with Baby Ross. "This baby has to be you. Look at all the red hair."

Ross laughed. "Yep, has to be me. I guess that's my mom. I never really knew her. She made choices that took her out of my life forever." He kissed her with growing intensity. "I missed you so much."

"I missed you too, but we're not married, you know." Dorie tried to pull away from him.

"A fact I suggested remedying, if you recall."

He kissed each of her fingertips, sending fire through her veins into her heart.

"No, Ross. This isn't what we want."

"Are you sure it's not what we want?" His eyes looked deep into her soul. "I want you in all the ways a man wants a woman, Dorie."

She jumped up from the lounge chair. "I want to wait for our wedding night."

Ross stood and captured her hands. "I understand. It's okay, I can wait. It's getting harder to hear you say 'no', though." He wrapped his arms around her and held her tightly to him. "Perhaps I should stay at Riley's. He could use the company, and we should avoid the temptation to go too far." Ross kissed her neck, sending chills down her spine.

"I don't want to kick you out of your own house. Maybe I should stay at the Andrews' cottage instead."

"No, I insist. I even know where he hides the key." Ross hugged her. "Don't worry. I'll be back. Let's make dinner first."

He kissed her sweetly, though she could still feel the heat in his lips. Ross scooped her up and carried her into the house to the kitchen. Dorie laughed as he stumbled over the threshold and nearly hit her head on the doorframe.

"You laughin' at me?" Ross hugged her tighter.

Dorie giggled louder. "I can't help it. Put me down, you big hunk of man."

"If we had a couch, I could put you down on it." Ross set her in a bistro chair. "You weigh nothing, girl."

"All I eat is chicken salad croissants and coffee at

Java Joint, when I actually eat."

"Do we even have food in the house?" Ross tilted his head. "That's it. I'm going for food. Burgers and fries?"

"Sure. I do have Coke and coffee."

"Good girl. I'll be right back. Call Melody's and tell her I'm coming." Ross grabbed the keys Grandpa's old truck, grabbed a quick kiss, and headed out the door. "While I'm gone, think on an earlier wedding date."

Chapter 14

Spending the night at Riley's …

Ross pulled his grandpa's old truck into Riley's driveway right behind Riley's cruiser. Riley was just getting out of the SUV.

"You just get back from Atlanta?" Ross reached his friend and gave him a handshake and bear hug.

"You get kicked out already?" Riley gave him a sad smile.

"Yes. Okay if I stay on your couch tonight?" Ross held the screen door while Riley fiddled with the key in the lock. "Figured you could use the company."

Riley opened the door and flipped on a light in the front room. "Come in. Nothing more I can do for my mom. How can I help you?"

"Just need Dorie to set an earlier wedding date, or I need to go back to California."

"Did she tell you I asked her if she was pregnant?" Riley dumped his coat on the recliner and headed into the kitchen. "Food?"

"I see how it is. I get kicked out because you asked her the one question you shouldn't have? Thanks, friend." Ross leaned against the wall in the kitchen.

"Food? Drink?" Riley leaned deep into the fridge. "Coke?"

"Sounds fine. Got any Cheetos?" Ross opened the pantry and rummaged. "Do you people ever go to the grocery?"

"Well, there's been a maniac on a rampage through town. It's kept everybody pretty busy." He handed Ross a Coke.

"Sorry about your mom." Ross pulled a bag of Cheetos out of the pantry. "You never disappoint, man. Pregnant, really? No wonder she didn't feel safe in the house with me there overnight. Thanks."

"My bad, dude. She was sick and peaked. I didn't know about Elliott."

Ross shook his head and plopped on the couch. "Relationships. They're tough."

After talking until midnight, Ross took the couch and Riley headed to bed.

Ross woke with a cough to a smokey haze. The smoke alarm was blaring.

"Riley? You okay? Wake up, dude." Ross headed toward Riley's bedroom.

Riley met him in the hall. "Get out! I'm right behind you." Ross caught a glimpse of his gun and badge in the waistband of his sweats.

Ross picked up his overnight bag and jacket and headed for the front door. Sirens screamed in the night toward them.

When he opened the door, a whoosh of air ignited the fire. The two men hurried onto the porch as the fire truck pulled up in front. Ross got a few steps from the house and dropped to his knees coughing. Riley joined him.

"Cap, what's going on? First your mom's house,

now yours. Don't suppose you saw anything, did you?

Riley shook his head. "I was asleep when I heard you yelling and the smoke alarm blaring. I bet it's the same person responsible, though." Coughing overwhelmed him with the effort of speaking.

Ross coughed while he pounded Riley on the back. "Out with the bad, in with the good."

The medics moved the men away from the house to the ambulance. Then they strapped oxygen masks on them. Both men were wrapped in blankets to protect against the October night and shock.

The house was fully engulfed before the fire fighters could set up. They fought to contain the fire.

"You okay, buddy?" Ross wrapped an arm around Riley while they watched his possessions burn to the ground.

"Ryker did this. Why is he so angry at me? We could have died tonight!" Riley shook with anger and the chill night air.

"If I know you and Dorie, you'll get to the bottom of this. Meanwhile, you can come sleep on my futon on the floor."

Riley and Ross watched until the fire crew finished putting out the blaze.

At three AM, Riley and Ross headed up the mountain to Helen.

***

When Dorie came downstairs, she found the living room floor full. The futon cushion had been pulled off its rickety frame and planted in the floor. Ross and Riley were both sprawled on the cushion but hugging the edges of it because Star was between them with legs in the air, "roaching" as it's called. Good thing Dorie was dressed.

She crouched down next to Ross and kissed him. "Sweetheart, what's going on? I thought you were sleeping over at Riley's. Instead it looks like the sleepover was here."

His eyes opened, and he began coughing. "Just smoke inhalation. Someone burned down Riley's."

Ross reached out for Dorie, pulled her onto the floor with him, and wrapped her in a sleepy bear hug. "This I could get used to.

"Who or what started the fire?"

"Who do you think?" The sleepy reply came from the other side of the dog. Riley started coughing too. "My vengeful lookalike, I'm sure."

At that, Star rolled over, stood up, stretched, and shook, causing her floormates to cry out in the commotion. Star headed for the door and barked until Ross stumbled to the door and let her out.

Dorie climbed off the floor and headed for the kitchen. "Coffee for everyone? Remember, I'm not Angela. I take limited requests." She could see through the window between the two rooms.

Riley sat up in the makeshift bed. "Do you make espresso black? I need to get back to town, find a uniform at the station, and make funeral arrangements."

Dorie started up the fancy machine. "Espresso black, coming up." Dorie backed up against the counter as the coffee drained into the cup.

Ross entered the kitchen and slipped both arms around her. "Good morning, fiancée."

"You smell like barbeque." Tears slipped down

her cheeks. "I should not have sent you away. You could have died, my love."

"Now, now, Dorie. No one could have foreseen Ryker burning Riley's house so soon after Mama Mary's death." Ross kissed her neck, her cheek, her lips. Then he wiped her tears with his hand.

Riley entered. "Coffee done?"

Ross released Dorie. She jumped away and got the cup for Riley.

"Guys, guys, guys. You are engaged. You're allowed to 'spark' in your own home." He took a sip. "Good coffee. I should invest in one of these machines."

Chapter 15

Funeral and fire lead to the suspect …

Dorie followed Riley and Ross into Daelin to Riley's burnt out shell of a home. They got out of their vehicles and walked over to the remains of the house. Dorie took out her notepad and took down observations. Greg drove up and started taking photos. The fire marshal, Marty, was already on site, examining the fire pattern.

"What have you found?" Riley called out to him. "What happened?"

"Come over here, Captain." Marty waved him over to the HVAC unit. "Whatchathink? See the burns. It looks like someone put additional fire to the gas line and ruptured it."

"Arson." Riley kicked a chunk of charred drywall. "Write it up, Marty. A copy on my desk as soon as possible."

"Gotcha, Captain." He clapped Riley on the back. "Glad you and Ross got out okay. This fire was meant to kill."

Riley nodded, and the fire marshal got in his Daelin FD Jeep and drove away.

"Can I go with you to help you with arrangements?" Ross stood beside him. "I was like your brother growing up. No one should bury his mother alone."

"Or with a vengeful brother?"

"No, I don't expect he'll be interested in helping with that. He's done enough already." Ross headed toward his truck. "I'll meet you there."

Dorie kissed Ross before he went to the station with Riley. She drove toward the *Beacon* to write about the latest exploits of Ryker Johnson.

"Lots of excitement at your house last night?" Ethan called out from the back of the office. "Come, tell me what you know. Did you talk to Marty?"

Dorie dumped her bag and computer at her desk and headed back to the editor's office.

"The fire marshal says it's arson, designed to kill Riley." Dorie put her hands through her hair. "He nearly killed Ross as well."

"Maybe that's not by accident." Greg entered and handed Dorie prints from the last batch of negatives. "Ross and Riley. Frick and Frack, so to speak. Ryker should have been Frick, not Ross."

Dorie looked at the photos. "Jealousy? Anger? He's gone off his rocker, killing people, burning homes down. Burglary is small stuff, comparatively."

Greg put his hand on her shoulder. "You're worried for good reason. Perhaps someone else should be trying to find this guy. The police, perhaps?"

Ethen laughed out loud. "Ah, the power of the fourth estate. To do the things the governors are unable to do. To shine light in dark places where no one dares to look."

"He's right. The man is running around Daelin in a purple Mustang. He shouldn't be so hard to find. Where can you hide a purple car?"

The clock on the wall ticked while the three thought.

"The dump. Where the hippy cars of the '60s and '70s have gone to rust away." Greg headed for his camera.

Dorie ran for her bags and computer. They both jumped into Greg's van and headed for the dump at the edge of town. On the way, Dorie alerted Riley.

Squad cars arrived as Dorie and Greg did. The police held them back while they did a search of the dump. Eventually a shrill whistle invited them to a spot on the edge of the field. A camp stove and chair sat sheltered by multicolored cars, Gremlins, Pacers, VW Beetles, and a hippie van straight from a Grateful Dead concert or Woodstock.

"Evidence someone has been living in this space. Perfect spot to hide a purple Mustang." Riley kicked an empty pork 'n' bean can. "Fingerprint the area. Leave it the way you found it. Then put a 24/7 surveillance on it. We must catch this man before he kills again.'

Greg began photographing the area.

"Greg, this is an ongoing investigation. I gotta ask you to share your photos with the crime lab and not publish anything about this in the *Beacon* until we run him to ground." Riley turned to Dorie. "Ditto, News Lady. I don't want him tipped off or spooked. No articles, not a word, about this site until he's caught."

Greg nodded. "You bet. Whatever we can do to help."

Dorie nodded while she took notes and sketched on her legal pad.

"Once we have what we need, we should vacate the premises as quickly as possible. We don't want a scared rabbit on the loose." Riley adjusted the collar of the extra uniform. "Oh, God, help me through it all."

"How can I help?" Dorie was close enough to hear his prayer.

"I need a dress for Mama for the funeral. Any chance you could take that off my plate?"

Dorie nodded.

Riley wiped his face. "Time. I need time."

Dorie took his hand. "By the way, you should take a look at these pictures. We don't think it was an accident that Ross was threatened by the fire."

He flipped through the pictures. "Yeah, so? It's me and Ross. We were like …" He squatted to the ground and held his head in his hand.

Dorie squatted beside him. "Brothers?"

Riley nodded. "I need to put a watch on Ross, too."

"Captain?" Sergeant Jones handed him a baby book. "I think this is one of the things your mother reported missing."

Riley paged through it. Page after page had been slashed. Pages with Ross slashed twice.

"Was it fingerprinted?"

The sergeant nodded.

"Put it back exactly as it was. We don't want him to know we were here." Riley looked around the campsite. "If you've done all you need to do, people, get out of here so Ryker Johnson will actually come back."

DIANE E. TATUM

Chapter 16

Leading to danger for everyone …

Dorie entered the sanctuary where Mama Mary's casket set at the front. Taped organ music played while participants spoke softly to prepare for the service. Ross and Riley sat in officiants' chairs on the dais. Both were dressed in brand new black suits and black shoes. Riley's had burned in the fire, and Ross's no longer fit due to his physical job out West. Dorie smiled. They both were so handsome. Her mom would say, "They clean up good."

Ross noticed her and ran down the aisle toward her. He took her into his muscular arms and squeezed her tight.

"So glad you're here, Sweetheart. I couldn't do this without you."

They kissed.

"Aren't there church laws about kissing in church? Like, aren't you supposed to be married?" Riley had followed Ross down the aisle as well with both hands in his pockets.

Dorie disentangled herself from Ross's grip, so she could hug Riley. "I am so sorry all this is happening to you. The man must be deranged from jealousy and rage."

"I know. I failed to protect Mama. I failed to protect my dog. I failed to protect Angela. And Ross and me, well, we were nearly killed as well." He hugged her. "You need to stay as far away from this as possible. I don't want you at risk again."

Ross tapped Riley on the shoulder, and he released Dorie.

"If Ross is in it, so am I." She shuddered as she realized the weight of those words. Perhaps they should already be married, in case one of them never lived that long. She grabbed Ross's and Riley's hands. "Three Musketeers?"

"One for all and all for one? Sounds about right." Angela had walked in, sporting a neon green cast. "Sorry, no coffee today, folks. At least not until after the funeral." She hugged each of them. "Closed casket?"

Riley nodded. "She wouldn't want to be remembered the way she ended up."

Dorie found a seat and watched the procession of people into the sanctuary, all 'huggin' their necks' and speaking a kind word. Most she didn't know. Some she knew by their names. Only a few people arrived with whom she had a true connection: folks from the *Beacon* and the police station, employees at Java Joint, spouses of some of them, Melody from the diner in Helen, a few from the church. Clearly Riley and Ross were strongly connected to just about everyone in Daelin and surrounds.

She turned around when the organist turned off the tape and started playing. Ross scooted in beside her on the second pew.

Riley sat up front alone. He turned around. "You two sit with me up here. You're more family than the psycho who caused this funeral."

Ross nodded, took Dorie's hand, and they changed seats to the front pew of the church.

When the pallbearers, all ranking police officers plus Ross, carried the casket to the waiting hearse, Dorie caught a flash of purple at the end of the parking lot.

What gall! Coming to the funeral of a woman he killed.

Riley snagged her arm. "I see him too. But I will not give him the satisfaction of disrupting my mother's funeral."

Ryker revved the engine, daring someone to come after him.

"Captain! Should we give chase?" Those officers not holding the casket questioned Riley.

"No. We'll get him when he least expects it."

"Are you sure, Riley?" Dorie squeezed his arm. "He could be willing to disrupt the procession."

"Let him try. We have a full police escort today. It'd be my pleasure to add disrespecting the dead and grieving to his growing list of crimes."

Once the casket was in the hearse, people loaded into their cars to follow it to the cemetery at the center of town.

When people arrived at the cemetery, instead of sitting in the rickety little folding chairs, they followed Riley's example, standing at the gravesite. Dorie wrapped her arm around him while the pallbearers carried Mama Mary to her resting place.

The men stood arm in arm with the rest of the mourners.

"Ashes to ashes, dust to dust." The pastor called out in the dreary day. "So, we have been, so we shall be."

"Amen," the crowd responded.

"God is Spirit and so is our sister, lovingly known by all as Mama Mary. Her Christian soul has joined God the Father, God the Son, and God the Holy Spirit in her eternal home. Those of us who are also Christians will one day see her again."

"Amen." The crowd murmured their response.

"Until that day, we bid you adieu, knowing it is not farewell as some might believe."

Tears ran down Dorie's cheeks, despite her efforts to be strong for Riley's sake. Ross pulled a pressed white hanky from his back pocket and put it into her hand. She nodded her thanks, and Ross squeezed her tighter around her waist. She leaned into his strong shoulder. Somehow the tears flowed faster. Not really for Mama Mary, but for all of them who had already lost so much in this year.

Riley squeezed her shoulders from the other side as the funeral workers lowered the coffin into the vault and sealed the lid atop it.

The funeral director then invited Riley and each of the pallbearers to add their own shovel of dirt to the grave.

Dorie stepped back from the grave to allow others access. She was really the interloper here, the newbie to the community. Her heels stuck in the loose soil, threatening to undo her balance, until she stepped onto the road leading to the grave.

That's when she heard the revving of a V8 engine. She looked up just in time to see the purple car peel out toward her.

Chapter 17

Fighting to find the man responsible …

In the seconds between the sound and the potential impact, Ross rushed the street, grabbed Dorie up in his arms, and both narrowly escaped bodily harm. The next thing she knew she was on the ground on the opposite side of the road from the grave with Ross on top of her.

"Are you okay?" He moved to help her off the ground. "All I could think was that he was going to hurt you, and I couldn't allow that to happen."

Dorie took Ross's hand to help her to her feet. She brushed the gravel and dirt from her skinned palms. When she looked back toward the crowd of mourners, Dorie realized everyone was watching her. Riley broke free from the crowd and ran to her side.

"Are you hurt? Good thing Ross thought quicker than I did." He clasped onto Dorie's arm.

Ross's arm around her waist pulled her closer to him. "Well, I have a lifelong stake in Dorie's well-being."

The funeral director appeared at Riley's elbow. "We're ready to close the grave, and you wanted to be present for that."

Riley nodded and released Dorie. "Can you both come and stand with me while the grave is closed?"

"I think I'll wait in the car, Ross. You go ahead." Dorie stumbled as she set out for the car. She hadn't realized until then that she was shaking. Luckily, her car was second in the procession line with only Riley's service vehicle and the hearse in front of hers. Ross's truck was back at the church.

Dorie climbed into the driver's seat and snagged a Kleenex from the box in the back seat to put between her palms. She didn't want to wipe blood on Ross's white hanky or on her good clothes. Her head began to pound, as well. She reclined her seat and closed her eyes.

When she woke, Dorie heard them fighting.

"You are putting Dorie at risk! She's doing your job! The entire police force has done less to find and identify this man than Dorie, a journalist, has done. Why don't you and your posse do your job?"

"This isn't the wild west, Ross. We can't just nab him and hang him. If I could find him, without others around, I'd probably give him the brotherly beat down he deserves, though." Riley walked away from Ross.

Ross reached out and grabbed Riley's shoulder. "I'm talking about Dorie's safety."

Riley turned around and threw an undercut to Ross's chin. Before long, it was a fist fight with police officers trying to pull them apart.

A rap at her car window startled Dorie. She rolled down the window.

"Think you can make them stop, ma'am. I think the fight is not about the man in the purple car. I think it's about you."

Dorie shook her head. "I don't think I'd know what to say." She opened the car door and climbed out onto the street any way.

Ross and Riley's fight had devolved into rolling around on the ground, hitting, slapping and wrestling by whoever was on top at the time. Those new black suits didn't have much chance of being worn again.

Dorie stood near them with hands on her hips. "Really, boys? How old are you two anyway?" She tapped her foot.

Ross stopped his punch in mid-air, allowing Riley to land his right hook. Riley stood and helped Ross up from the ground. Both made attempts to straighten and brush the dirt from their suits.

"Do you really think Mama Mary would find this an appropriate way of remembering her after she's barely buried?" Dorie crossed her arms. "I think not. I'm headed back to the office. You two work it out like professionals. I'll see you back up on the mountain unless you decide you both need other accommodations." Dorie turned and headed for her car.

Ross followed Dorie to her car. Dorie got in and locked the doors. "Get a ride back to the church with someone else."

He clambered into Riley's service vehicle just before the procession line began to move toward the exit.

***

Ross couldn't believe Dorie made him ride back with Riley after that fist fight.

"Well?" Riley turned out of the cemetery toward

97

the church.

"Well, what? You took the first swing." Ross could feel the ire rising into his face again. "Dorie is my fiancée. I just want her safe. What is wrong with you?"

"What do you think is wrong? I just buried my mother whom my long-lost twin brother killed." Riley turned left into the church parking lot. "He also burned down my childhood home, and my current home is also in ashes. You've been like a brother to me my entire life. We could have died in that housefire." Riley pulled the SUV next to Ross's truck.

"What's that got to do with Dorie? I can tell you're in love with her. So can Ryker, that's why he's targeting her too."

"Well, you get engaged then fly away to California. She's lonely and alone, especially up on the mountain. What are you doing to keep her safe?"

Riley's accusation cut right to Ross's gut. "You're right. Until she tells me differently, though, she's my fiancée. Don't use her and put her in danger."

Riley nodded. "Agreed. But she is kinda headstrong."

"It's one of the things I love about her." Ross got out of the car. "Are you coming up the mountain to sleep on my floor?"

"Probably." Riley nodded. "I would never put Dorie in danger on purpose. You know that, right?"

"I know. Because you're in love with her." Ross grinned. "Don't forget I am, too."

"Got it." Riley put his car in Drive as his radio began squawking. "I better go see what this is about."

Ross closed the door and waved as Riley headed out across the parking lot. When his captain's service vehicle hit the street, his sirens and flashing lights signaled he was on his way to an emergency. Ross shook his head, climbed into his truck, and headed for the *Beacon* offices or Java Joint to try to smooth everything out with Dorie.

Dorie's blue compact car was at Java Joint. That was a good thing for Ross. She'd be less likely to yell at him in public.

Ross pulled the truck up next to her car, then headed inside.

"Double shot espresso with foam, unless California has you drinking some soymilk invention." Angela handled the espresso, even with a neon green cast.

"Nah, same order as always, Angie. Looks like you're still able to operate with the cast." Ross leaned on the counter while she worked. "Sounds like it's been nightmarish around here."

"'cept for the broken arm, I'm good. Now Riley is a different story, but I guess you knew that. Sounds like if it weren't for you, Riley would be having a funeral for himself."

"It was a God thing. I just woke up at the right time." He pointed heavenward.

"Sounds like Ryker is wanting to make Riley miserable. Heard about your heroics at the cemetery. Nice save."

"Guess you heard about the fight as well, huh?" Ross took his wallet out and paid for the drink. "Ryker tried to run Dorie over."

"Crazy business, isn't it? She's at the regular

table." Angela handed him his cup and pointed toward the back. "Here's pastry, on the house."

"Thanks." Ross balanced the coffee and two plates, and he walked toward Dorie's office at Java Joint. "Can I join you?"

Dorie looked into his eyes. "If you have something to say. Otherwise, I've got work to do."

"Ah, Dorie. You know I love you." He placed the plates on the table, then sat across from her with his coffee. "I just think Riley has crossed a line while I've been in California. Am I wrong?"

"He's been a good friend while this craziness has gone on." Dorie looked up from her laptop. "You haven't been here to know what's been happening."

Ross raised his hands in surrender. "Guilty as charged. Second time in the last hour, in fact. Still, I trust our bond. I trust you. Riley has fallen for you. I recognize the signs."

"Don't you see?" Dorie reached across the table and took Ross's hand. "It doesn't matter whether he loves me or not. It only matters that I love you, and you love me."

Ross moved over to sit beside her. "What about Riley?"

"He's our friend. We help him, whatever he needs from us. Fighting with him at the cemetery, not a good move." Dorie kissed his cheek. "Riley's world is crashing around him, not to mention he has an evil twin. You have everything, he's lost it all."

Ross felt the blood rush to his face. "You're right. He needs us both. How are you so wise?"

"How are you so lucky that I picked you?"

"I'm not lucky. It's a God thing." Ross wrapped

his arms around her and kissed her. "And I have a coffee-stained tie to prove it."

"Break it up, lovers. No PDAs in the Java Joint." Angela slapped the table. "You got a better place to make up than here."

Dorie's laugh put Ross at ease. "I love you."

Dorie kissed him. "I know. Grab pizza for the three of us your way back home."

Chapter 18

Conspiracy at foot …

Dorie dropped in at the police station before heading up the mountain.

"Hey, Miss Dorie. You okay? That was a tough save at the cemetery." Sgt. Stevens greeted her at the desk. "I don't think I ever saw Ross MacAvoy move that fast."

She rubbed her shoulder. "I will feel it tomorrow. Is Captain McDonough in?"

Sgt. Stevens nodded and buzzed on the intercom. "Cap, Miss Dorie is here. You available?"

"Send her back, Sarge."

"Go on back."

Dorie nodded and headed to Riley's office. Riley met her at the door with a hug.

"I need to apologize, Dorie. I took the first swing at Ross. This fight wasn't his fault." He indicated the chair in front of his desk. "Don't give him a hard time. I was raw."

"Why aren't you taking the day off?" Dorie sat on the edge of the seat and set her backpack down beside her. "Your house burned down, and your mom's funeral was today. Surely those things allow you time to recover."

Riley plopped into his office chair. "Where? There's nowhere to go. Until we catch Ryker, I need to stay vigilant."

"You are welcome at the house. Ross and I expect you for pizza later and a place on the living room floor. Consider taking tomorrow off and hanging out on the mountain."

"Thanks. I'll think on it. I sure don't want anything to happen to Ross's grandparents' home though because I'm there."

"Nonsense. Pizza at six."

***

After Dorie left, Riley met with the shift coming on duty. Once they settled, Riley handed out duty assignments.

"Robinson and St. Johns, relieve Smith and Thomas staking out the junk yard. Ryker Johnson has to come back to his makeshift home at some point. Pearson, take Richards and stakeout my burned-out house in case Johnson returns there. Manning and Henderson, stakeout Java Joint. Keep Angela and her customers safe. Stevens, get Helen PD on the phone. I need officers on Ross MacAvoy's house through morning. The rest of you, patrol your normal routes. Not too many purple cars roam our streets. If you must, pull over every single one. If the driver looks like me, lock him up." Riley paused, allowing the emotions boiling over in him to subside. "I don't have to tell you that this is important and personal to me. But this man's actions don't only harm my family, they also put the whole community in jeopardy."

A hand went up in the back.

"Yeh, Hardeman?"

"Maybe I read too many crime novels, but what if he were to kidnap you and take your place as captain, like not kill you but takeover your life?"

Laughter tinged with desperation succeeded his suggestion, though Riley didn't laugh. It was almost too possible.

"Hardeman, see me after dismiss. Any questions? You have a picture profile. You'll know him when you see him. He's lived a much tougher life than I have. Dismissed."

In the ruckus of shift change, Hardeman approached the podium.

"Cap, you wanted to see me? I wasn't making fun of the situation."

Riley took a deep breath. "It's just so crazy, it might just happen. I'm putting you in charge of questioning my identity. This is between you and me, Joe. If you think I seem off or don't look or act like myself, I want you to say to me 'Gemini.' If it's actually me, I'll answer 'conspiracy'. Understand?"

"You sure, Cap?" Hardeman pulled at his shirt collar.

Riley nodded. "Yes. If I don't answer correctly, handcuff the man and lock him up. Then find me."

"That's a lot of responsibility, Riley. I mean, Captain."

"You're right, it is. I'm putting my faith in you. We may be depending on you to protect our community from my brother."

"Yes, sir." Hardeman saluted and turned to take his shift.

Riley walked back to his office. *What a day. I*

buried my mother. Fought my best friend. Insulted the girl I love, whom I shouldn't love. And sent out an APB on my twin brother. Lord, protect us all from Ryker's vengeful plan.

Riley plopped into his desk chair. The clock on the wall ticked off the seconds. He had to leave for Helen soon if he was going to get any pizza at Ross and Dorie's. Ross and Dorie's. He needed to let go the hope of Dorie being interested in him as more than a friend. And that just made his heart hurt. He leaned back in the swivel chair and closed his eyes. *Lord, what a mess this is.*

"Captain?"

Riley opened his eyes. "Yes, Sergeant?"

"Helen PD is setting up protection detail at the MacAvoy place immediately. I put out the APB on the purple car with warnings to approach with caution. The officers have changed shifts. Anything else I can do for you before I go?"

"No. Go home to your wife, Stevens. Good work."

After Sergeant Stevens saluted and left, Riley stood, stretched, and pulled on his coat and hat. Time to make the trip up the mountain. *Lord, why isn't it easy?*

***

Dorie strained to see through the rain to the main road. A visible police presence had set a perimeter around the house, no doubt Riley's doing. "He will come, won't he?"

Ross put ice in glasses. "Sure. Where else can he go? Miss Daisy's Motel is ok for a night, but not as home."

The timer dinged. Frozen pizza was ready, but no

sign of Riley.

"Should I pour our drinks? It's nearly 6:30. The pizza won't keep too long." Ross came to Dorie and put his arms around her. "Have I told you today how much I love you?"

Dorie relaxed in his arms. "Yes, but the pizza is going to burn."

"I suppose 'let it burn' is not the appropriate response at this time." Ross nuzzled into her neck making her giggle.

"No. Burnt pizza is right up there with burnt popcorn and burnt cookies." Dorie ducked under his arms to rescue the pizza. "And it's almost there. Call Riley and see where he is." She grabbed the hot mitts and pulled the pizza stones from the oven.

Ross called him. "It's Ross calling to remind you of your dinner and boarding reservation in Helen, Georgia, for tonight. Call me back. We're getting worried."

Headlights flashed across the kitchen window.

Ross headed for the front door. "That must be him. I'll see if I can help him with baggage or something."

Dorie looked out the window. Riley's captain's vehicle had parked in the gravel drive. She watched him take out a cup carrier of drinks, probably coffee, and distribute them to one patrol car to the next. Ross followed him with a second tray. Then Riley grabbed fast food bags from his car and handed them out to the police officers guarding the house. Once every officer had been served, Ross and Riley jogged through the rain to the front door.

"That was so sweet, Riley." Dorie hugged his neck. "Would you like a towel to dry off?"

Ross appeared from the downstairs bath with a towel as she spoke. "I'm ahead of you on that one, Sweetheart."

While both men dried their hair and clothes as best as they could, Dorie completed the preparations for dinner. "Come and get it. Afraid the old futon and a coffee table is the best we have to eat on. Self-serve. I'll turn on a movie."

"What's the movie tonight?" Riley draped the towel over the banister.

Ross grabbed his towel and Riley's and took them to the downstairs bath. "Monty Python and the Holy Grail."

"Well, why not? That's about the way this day has gone."

Chapter 19

Praying for resolution …

Ross rounded up the popcorn bowls and napkins. Dorie picked up the paper plates and glasses.

"Thanks, guys. It's been a while since I laughed so hard. How can I help?" Riley leaned against a corner of hallway.

"Put down the futon. You can sleep there tonight. I'm going to bring in a chaise lounge from the deck to sleep on." Ross slapped Riley on the back. "Maybe we'll both get some sleep that way."

"Why don't we pray before bed? God has the answer to this situation." Dorie held out a hand to each of them.

"I'll pray." Ross grabbed Riley's hand to complete the circle. "Holy Father, Thank you for your protections of today. Help the police find Ryker Johnson before he hurts anyone else. Protect Riley, my best friend and brother, from the evil schemes of his twin. Give us a good night of sleep, so we can meet the challenges of tomorrow. Amen."

Tears ran down Riley's face. "Thanks."

Ross gave Dorie a chaste kiss before she headed upstairs. While he and Riley arranged their sleeping options, Ross found a blanket for Riley's bed and drug the chaise in from the deck. The rain fell harder, and the wind whistled at the windows of the cottage on the mountain.

Just after they turned out the lights, lightning lit the room followed by an immediate crash of thunder. The nightlight in the hall went out. Without the hum the refrigerator, computers, and the HVAC, the house was silent.

Riley's walkie squawked. "Captain McDonough, you there?"

"I'm here. What's happening?"

"Lightning hit the transformer here in Daelin. We're in the dark. The emergency generator is handling dispatch."

"Do I need to come? You know I'm in Helen."

Ross opened the front door. The rain was so dense he couldn't see the police cruisers at the road. One came into view and pulled up to the porch.

A burly police officer Ross had known all his life hurried up onto the porch. "We've been pulled off protective detail for now. That lightning blew the transformer and started a fire down at the old Welch place."

"It's okay, Bobby. It's too bad a night for anyone to be out making mischief. Mother Nature has that covered."

Another bright flash followed by a loud boom made both men jump.

Dorie rushed down the stairs, tying her robe on the way. "What's going on?" Dorie peeked around Ross. "Everything okay?"

"I'll be going then, Ross, ma'am." Bobby hustled

out to his car and threw it into Reverse.

Ross turned and moved Dorie back into the house. "You shouldn't be parading around in your night clothes. You're awful hard to resist as it is."

A flashlight popped on. "I'm gonna have to head down to Daelin." Riley frightened them both. "The town is in the dark. With Ryker stalking us, I better see how I can help comfort people." He laughed. "This is a touching sight, both of you in bedclothes. I'm saying, you two need to go ahead and get married. Thanks for the hospitality. I'll probably sleep in the bunks at the station."

"Be safe." Dorie hugged him. "The weather is atrocious."

"Maybe you should both ride down with me." Riley kissed her cheek. "As a friend, Ross."

"I just got Star settled in her crate. We don't need electricity to sleep." Dorie kissed his cheek. "Go on. We'll see you in the morning, sooner if there's not electricity for coffee."

Riley headed out in the rain to his service vehicle. His headlights swept the front yard. No police cars remained.

"Guess we're on our own." Ross looped his arm around her. "Riley might be right about going on and getting married." He kissed her with growing passion.

Dorie was the one who broke the kiss. "I'll sleep on it. Good night, my love."

Ross wanted to follow her up those stairs. He wanted her, needed her, in every way imaginable. But he also wanted her to be safe, to be loved, to be who God wanted them both to be. He could wait, though it was sometimes very difficult. Nearly impossible, at other times.

***

Riley careened down the mountain in the storm. Dispatch crackled constantly with emergencies all over the area. Situations everywhere sounded dire. It was hard enough worrying about what Ryker might do next. Now the entire county was in uproar. The flashing lightning and rumbling thunder jarred his nerves. The road was slick and curvy. He could barely see through the rain and the wiper swipes.

Around a dangerous curve, Riley spotted the purple car off the side of the road, angled down toward the ravine. He pulled his service vehicle to the side of the road and jumped out of the SUV into the storm. He slid down the edge, catching the car on the way down.

"Ryker!" Riley wrenched open the passenger door. "Are you okay?"

Ryker was slumped over the steering wheel, bleeding from his head. Riley tried to climb into the front seat. The car shifted with his weight on the door. He backed away and climbed back up to his car.

"Dispatch, Captain McDonough here. I need an ambulance and a tow truck on the road between Helen and Daelin ASAP. I found Ryker Johnson and the stolen purple car, off the road. I need a patrol car here as well."

"10-4, Captain. Ambulance, tow truck, and patrol car on their way to your location ASAP."

The rain became torrential. Riley stood at the road edge and watched the cliffside wash downhill. The car slipped further toward the ravine. His heart was torn. His brother. A murderer, arsonist, assaulter, and thief. A violent man who shared the same mother, the same womb, the same DNA, the same face. Perhaps he'd felt his loss, so some said. Ross had filled that spot throughout their childhood. What did this man mean to him?

The flashing lights appeared in the distance. Soon the tow truck had the car hooked to its wench. Fighting the deepening mud, the purple car inched up the slippery surface until it was at an angle with the road.

Riley moved his SUV to give the tow truck more room to maneuver the car onto the road. The ambulance stood by waiting to care for the man inside. The patrol car waited to keep the man in their custody.

"Captain, come sit in the ambulance and dry out a bit. You are drenched through and freezing. You don't need to get ill as well with what all's been going on."

"No, thank you, Paul. I need to see this through. Then I'll head back to Daelin PD, get a warm shower, and a set of sweats. You just take care of my brother."

The EMT nodded and stood with him as the purple Mustang rose back onto the road. The patrolman directed any traffic around the site. Once the car was safely on the road, EMTs surrounded it to get Ryker Johnson out and into the ambulance.

"How is he?" Riley peered in on him, his first true look at his identical twin.

"Concussion probable, some cuts and contusions. No worse for wear, I suspect. Need to get him imaged and checked over though. You know the drill." Paul shook Riley's hand. "We'll get him down to the hospital and let the docs take a look."

"I'll drive down behind you." Riley motioned for the patrolman to come over. "This man is under arrest the second he becomes conscious. Handcuff him to the bed. Do not, under any circumstances, let this man escape. Do you understand, Henry?"

Henry saluted and got back into the patrol car.

The flashing, screaming procession of ambulance, Riley's SUV, and Henry's patrol car headed down the curving mountain road to Daelin Medical Center. The tow truck brought up the rear with Dr. Eminem's electric purple Mustang.

Chapter 20

Keeping the twins identified …

W e came as soon as we could." Ross and Dorie hurried to Riley's side.

"Waiting outside another hospital room." Riley's hair was still damp from his shower. His Daelin PD sweats substituted for his normal clothing under the circumstances.

"Has he come to?" Dorie took his hand. "Is he badly injured?"

"Brought you some spare clothes. How are you feeling?" Ross handed him a bag with jeans and a tee shirt. "Hope they fit you okay, at least till you can go shopping."

"Thanks, brother. You know, this man may be my biological brother, but you and me, we are always connected in a way no other two persons could be." Riley hugged Ross. "I'm stunned and shaken. How can I have a twin and not know him? How can he be so different?"

Ross sat down and pulled Riley down beside him. "It's the eternal question, isn't it? Nurture vs. nature. Mama Mary took care of us. She made sure we were well-loved and cared for. For whatever reason, Ryker got the short end of the stick."

"What happened? How did my twin end up in foster care?" Riley held his head in his hands. "He's right. It's not fair."

Dorie put her arm around his shoulders. "I'm still trying to find out what happened."

Patrolman Joe Hardeman exited the hospital room. "Cap, Mr. Johnson is awake. I read him his rights and put him under arrest, like you said to. I'll wait here outside the door while you talk with him. If you need me, just yell."

"You guys go on and do what you need to do. It'll be light soon." Riley hugged them each and said good-byes.

"Let me know if you need me, brother." Ross slapped his back before guiding Dorie out to the car.

***

Riley entered the room. "So, we finally meet face to face." While the man looked similar to him, Dorie and Angie were right. Ryker's face showed the harder life he'd led. "Do you know why Mama thought you were dead?"

"Wishful thinking." His voice was coarse, a smoker's voice. "Hard enough raising one son without a dad." He turned and faced the wall.

"You killed our mom, burned down both her place and mine, nearly ran over Dorie at the cemetery, broke Angie's arm at Java Joint, burglarized the records office, and poisoned my dog. Why?" Riley wiped his sweaty palms on the Daelin PD sweatpants. He sat down next to the bed nearest the handcuffs. "I knew nothing about you until we traced the purple car back to UGA."

"And it would still be that way if I hadn't come back here. Poisoning your dog was low, I reckon. I wanted to get your attention though."

Riley willed his ire to go back to the pit of his stomach. Arguing with this man would do no one any good. "Well, you have my attention. Why do you want it?"

"It started out, I was looking for my biological mother, the one that gave me up. Imagine how surprised I was to find out she'd kept you and not me." He snorted. "My temper is not my best trait."

"On her dying breath, she swore she thought you had died. Dorie's still doing some investigating on what happened." Riley wanted to reach out to him but reminded himself that the handcuffs were for his own protection because Ryker was a criminal.

"Doesn't matter now, does it?" The man squirmed. "How long I gonna to be here? Might as well get it over with. Send me back to jail where I belong."

"So, you're planning to plead guilty?" Riley sighed. That would make things easier than a protracted court case.

The man shrugged. "Can't see how I can plead otherwise."

A nurse walked in with medicine and a syringe. "Sorry, Captain. I need to give my patient the meds that were finally approved."

"That's fine." Riley stood. "I'll check in on you later."

"Needn't bother with me now, Captain McDonough. I'll be outta your hair soon enough." Ryker stared at him. "You can forget me once you put me away. You shoulda just let me die in that ravine."

The nurse shushed Riley out of the room. He sent Joe Hardeman back in to watch over the bitter, hardened brother he never knew he'd had.

***

After a coffee and pastry at Java Joint, Ross dropped Dorie at the *Beacon*. She had to write up an article on the capture of the wanted fugitive, finish those negatives, finish the albums she'd promised, and figure out what happened to put Ryker in foster care.

"I'll be back for you later, darling." Ross shouted through the open window. "Let me know if I need to come by sooner."

"I will, Ross. I think I've got enough on my plate for now." Dorie waved until he was out of sight, then entered the offices in the strip mall.

"As a reporter, you're not supposed to be in the news." Ethan called out to her as the bell on the door dinged. "Got an article about the car in the ravine?"

"Writing it now, boss." Dorie lugged the backpack into the chair and pulled out the laptop and her notepad.

***

Ross headed over to the police station to check on Riley after a stop at Java Joint for Riley's espresso and a croissant."

"Richie Stevens! I haven't seen you in a month of forevers." Ross stuck out his hand to the desk sergeant.

"Hey, that's Sgt. Stevens in this building." He grabbed Ross's hand and pumped it. "What are you doing here? Delivery for Angela now?"

Ross laughed. "Nah. Hoping to catch Riley, excuse me, the Captain."

"I think he's in the bunk room. This situation with Ryker Johnson is too much for anybody to handle." Stevens pointed back to the maze of corridors and offices. "Head back to his office. You can see the break room from there. The bunk room is off to the left of the break room."

"Good to see you, Sergeant. We should get together." Ross grinned at his friend.

"Didn't I hear you're engaged to Dorie, the reporter?"

"Yes, still need to decide on a date for that wedding. Sooner is better than later, if you know what I mean."

Stevens laughed. "Before I even knew she was in town, you'd already snagged her. Way to go, MacAvoy!"

Ross cringed at the suggestion of impropriety after all the ways they'd continued to remain pure before their wedding. The world assumed they'd given in. "I'll go find the captain before his coffee gets cold."

He wandered back to Riley's office, then to the breakroom where he left the coffee and croissant. Then he headed back to the bunks.

"Riley." Ross whispered. If Riley was sound asleep, he wouldn't wake him.

"Do you know how hard it is to sleep in a place that operates twenty-four hours a day?" Riley grumbled and rolled over. "Can I help you?"

Ross grimaced. "I didn't want to wake you. Sorry."

"Wasn't asleep anyway. What's up?" Riley threw off the blanket and sat up on the side of the bed.

"I brought you coffee and a croissant from Java Joint. It's in the breakroom." Ross sat on a chair between the beds.

"That may be the best news I've heard in a while." Riley stood and stretched. "Let's go get that coffee."

Ross and Riley had no sooner sat down at the bistro type table in the break room when Sgt. Stevens came running in.

"Captain, sir, Ryker Johnson has escaped from his hospital bed. He slipped his cuffs and assaulted a nurse and an orderly. Patrolman Hardeman was knocked unconscious with something." He stood before them, breathless. "Orders, sir?"

Riley sighed. "Catch him, then lock him up so he can't escape."

"Yes, sir, Captain." Stevens ran back down the hallway, relaying the captain's orders.

Chapter 21

Deciphering the records …

D orie sat at a table in the hospital archives, basement actually, with stack of logbooks from the years around Riley, Ryker, and Ross's births. She pulled out her backpack and searched for the copy of the card she had taken from the Records Office the night of the burglary. She pulled the crumpled paper from the bottom of the bag.

Live birth: Ross Andrew MacAvoy
Date: May 20, 1990
Mother: Jeanine Annabelle Ross MacAvoy
Father: Andrew Glen MacAvoy
Daelin Medical Center, Daelin Georgia

His little baby footprint was stamped beside the bare information about the man she planned to marry. He never talked about his parents. Nor did he talk about his grandparents except his grandfather who had owned the house in Helen. Didn't she have the right to know about his family?

The siren startled her, then the emergency lights began flashing. The PA intoned, "Lockdown Protocol, Lockdown Protocol. All patients should remain in their rooms. All visitors remain where you are. Lockdown Protocol, Lockdown Protocol."

Ryker. It was the first word that popped into her head. *If he has escaped, no one in Daelin is safe. He wouldn't think to find her in the basement of the hospital, would he? Surely, they would catch him before he had a chance to find her here.*

The announcement continued. Dorie decided that staying in the basement was a better idea than taking a chance of meeting a desperate Ryker face-to-face. She cracked open the thirty-year-old volume. She sneezed and coughed at the dust escaping the crackling pages.

Dorie checked her notes on her laptop. The missing cards fell in Gemini between mid-May and mid-June. She ran her finger down the pages marked May. First, she saw Ross's entry: Jeanine MacAvoy admitted on May 19. Ross Andrew MacAvoy admitted to nursery on May 20. Both released on May 25. Then Riley's record: May 27, Mary McDonough admitted to maternity. May 28 Riley and Ryker McDonough admitted to hospital nursery. All released to home on June 3. As she turned the page, another entry caught her eye. June 6, Ryker McDonough admitted to hospital nursery. No date of release was recorded.

Dorie went back to the dusty shelves, looking for hospital nursery records or patient files. She found a bound volume marked Nursery Notes 1990. She pulled it off the shelf and sneezed violently with the resulting dust storm. Dorie lugged it toward her worktable when the door burst open. She crouched, hoping whoever it was wouldn't notice anyone here. *The computer's on!*

"Is someone here?" The voice was male and raspy. "I see your bag and computer, Dorie. Convenient to have your name on the strap."

Dorie feared the dust would give her away while clutching the important volume. She slowed her breathing as much as she knew how. She recalled the incident with Hilde. Hilde had killed Trudy over the former mayor's attentions. Dorie had come too close to an overdose of ketamine before Hilde shot herself rather than be captured. Dorie had survived that. Surely, she'd survive this too. His footsteps walked the length of the basement and back to the worktable. Then she heard the computer hit the concrete floor and the ruffle of papers flying from the table.

Finally, he stomped to the door, flung it open, and thumped up the stairs.

Dorie had nearly passed out from holding her breath. She took a deep breath as the door clicked back in place. Dorie waited a few more minutes before standing up. When she stood, her left foot had gone numb. She stumbled, nearly dropping the book. She hobbled to the worktable to assess the damage to her laptop and retrieve her notes.

The computer screen was shattered, and the housing was loose. She closed it and slid it into her backpack. She gathered the papers strewn to the air like leaves on an autumn day then stuffed them into the backpack along with the 1990 Nursery Notes. Dorie grabbed her phone from her jacket pocket and dialed Riley.

When he answered, she coughed. "Riley, Ryker is not cuffed to his bed anymore. He was just in the hospital basement where I am."

"Are you okay? Did he hurt you?" Riley's voice was full of panic. "A team of officers are searching floor by floor. I'll send them to you."

"He didn't find me, but he swiped my laptop off the table onto the concrete floor."

"I'll call Ross and send him to get you home. I have an APB out on Ryker. He can't get far without a car."

Riley hung up on her.

In seconds, Ross's text arrived. "Meet me at front entrance to the Center. Be careful!"

Dorie headed for the door with her belongings. As she reached for the door handle, the door flew open. The doorframe was filled with officer blue uniforms. Dorie clasped her mouth to hold in the scream that threatened to escape.

"Dorie Hudson? I'm Officer Johnny Martin. Have you seen Ryker Johnson?"

"No, but I heard him and saw the results of his anger when he didn't find me." Dorie described what had happened then headed up the steps to find Ross. Officer Martin accompanied her to the front entrance to stand with her.

The wind had turned cold while Dorie had been in the hospital basement. She buttoned her jean jacket up to her chin and stuffed her hands in the pockets.

Soon a bright blue new SUV with dealer plates pulled up. The passenger window descended. Her broad-shouldered, red-headed, outdoorsman was in the driver's seat.

"Hop in, let's head for Helen."

Dorie climbed in. "Where's your truck?"

"I left it at the car dealer. We're going to go pick it up. We've got this vehicle for the week. What do you think?"

"Are we trading in my car or your truck?" Dorie ran her hand over the creamy leather upholstery.

"Neither unless we decide to do so." Ross guided the vehicle into the car dealership and climbed out. He opened Dorie's door. "You drive it up the mountain road, and I'll follow with the truck."

"What about Ryker?" Dorie's voiced registered a little higher than she normally sounded. "My computer is smashed, too."

"Sounds like we need to buy a new one." Ross held the driver's door open for her. "Let's go home and plan our next move."

Dorie faced him. "What about Ryker?"

Ross kissed her. "Let's let the police worry about Ryker and Riley for a change."

Chapter 22

Making decisions …

Dorie and Ross were just finishing their Chinese takeout when Riley stumbled in.

"Hey, guys! I finally went shopping for clothes. I'll return yours, Ross, once I wash them." He set crinkly shopping bags down in the foyer.

"I can easily wash them with our clothes." Dorie set a place for him on the bistro table and gathered the leftover takeout boxes around his plate. "I think there's enough for you here."

"If not, I bet there's microwave popcorn. Right?"

Before Dorie could reply, Ross dove into the pantry and pulled out a wrapped popcorn packet. "Here you go, bro."

"I shouldn't have to crash here much longer. I've got a month to month lease on one of those townhomes where you each lived. I'll pick up some furniture and move in what little I have left tomorrow." Riley dumped the remaining fried rice onto his plate then added the beef and broccoli and honey chicken. "Thanks for taking care of me. I know the furniture's a little sparse here too."

Ross perched against the granite counter. "Actually, I had a call today to return to California.

The fires have died down, and the rangers are back in the forest doing clean up."

They're both going to leave me up here alone when there's a deranged murderer on the loose? Dorie turned away and found her backpack. She slid out the laptop, set it on the coffee table, and sat on the floor. While the men talked in the kitchen about leaving her, Dorie powered it up to see if she could download the contents onto her flash drive. The shattered screen slit her finger as she attempted to press the shards back in place. A large drop of blood fell onto the keyboard. *Darn!*

"Need this?" Ross offered her his handkerchief. "What are you doing?"

Exhaustion overwhelmed her. "Trying to salvage my work."

"Why don't you go on to bed? You're obviously tired. I'll see if I can get your files." Ross knelt beside her and kissed her. "If I can't, there's a guy in Daelin that can work magic on technology." He sat and gathered her into his lap.

"When are you leaving?" Her voice was small and shaky.

Ross pulled her closer. "Tomorrow. You can drive the SUV through the week. If you want it, the paperwork just needs your signature. The money's available as soon as you sign the documents. If you don't want it, return it and get someone to drive you back to your car."

"I'll be in St. Louis for Thanksgiving. Will you come?"

"It's a priority to meet your parents and brothers. Yes, I'll be there." He kissed Dorie's head. "Then we'll set our wedding date. Whenever you want it to be."

"Guess tomorrow is too soon then." Dorie snuggled into his shoulder.

"You're the one who wanted me to meet your family first."

Dorie sighed. "Tonight, that doesn't seem necessary to me."

"Sleep on it." Ross helped her up. "Tomorrow we'll talk about it again."

The poppity-pop and smell of microwave popcorn came from the kitchen.

"You sleep, I'll care for our guest and Star." Ross kissed her good night with promise of another night when they wouldn't have to sleep alone.

***

Ross watched her ascend the stairs alone. How badly he wished he could join her, even if it was just to cuddle and console her.

"Popcorn?" Riley appeared at his elbow with a mixing bowl full of buttery goodness. "We could watch a movie. Did Dorie cash in already?"

Ross sat back on the floor in front of the smashed computer. "Sure, you choose. I need to see if I can resurrect this computer enough to get all of Dorie's notes, articles, and ideas onto a flash drive."

"Jared in town can do it. What happened?"

"Ryker Johnson came into the hospital archives while Dorie was there. Luckily, he didn't find her. He did find her computer and notes and swiped them all onto the concrete floor."

"Is she okay?"

Ross shrugged. "I guess as can be expected."

"He'll run out of places to hide." Riley tossed back some popcorn. "How 'bout *Tombstone*? 'I'll be your Huckleberry.'"

"Sure thing. Pop it in." Ross shook his head. "At least there'll be justice at the end."

As the credits rolled on the movie, Riley snored away on the futon. Ross covered him with a blanket. Then he crept up the creaky stairs to check on Dorie.

The quiet regular breathing assured him that she was asleep. He reached in and flipped off the light.

"If only I could crawl in beside you and keep you safe in my arms." Ross closed the door and headed back downstairs.

As he locked the front door, Ross saw a flashlight beam sweep the front room. He threw the door open and saw a dark figure running toward the road. Ross ran after the man while dialing 911. "Yeah, I have an intruder on my property."

"Is anyone harmed, sir?"

"No, but we've been under protective detail due to the APB from Daelin for Ryker Johnson."

"Yes, sir. Can you confirm that the intruder was Ryker Johnson?"

Ross stood at the edge of the road, looking up and down. "No. I didn't see his face, and I don't see anyone now."

"I'll send a car by. For now, sir, I'd return to your home and lock the door. Call us back if the intruder returns."

"Got it. Just remember, this guy burns down houses with people inside them."

"Yes, sir. The officers will be sure to check around

your house when they arrive in just a few minutes."

Ross shook his head. "Okay." *Hope nothing burns down or explodes in the meantime.* He headed back to the house and locked the front door behind him. While he waited for the police to arrive, he doublechecked the other doors to the house.

The knock at the front door woke Riley. "What's happening?"

"It's Helen PD. We've had a visitor."

Ross opened the front door. Blue lights strobed across the front yard.

"What's happening?" Dorie came down the stairs. "Why are the police here? Ryker?"

"Ross MacAvoy? Are you the caller?"

"Yep, it's me."

Riley grabbed the door and opened it wider. "And I'm Captain McDonough of Daelin PD. Is there a problem here?" He headed out the door.

"No, sir. We'll check the property."

When Ross turned away from the door and closed it, Dorie sat on the stairs in her nightgown and robe, weeping. "Ah, darling. Don't cry." He sat down on the step and wrapped an arm around her.

Chapter 23

Cornering the twin …

Dorie slipped down the stairs in the half-light of dawn. She needed a new computer, her paper notes reorganized, and negatives identified. Plus, she'd be taking Ross to the Atlanta airport. No telling how much more mayhem would occur.

Ross was up, putting the chaise lounge back on the deck, blankets neatly folded on the futon. Riley had apparently never returned in the night. The futon was set up to be a couch again, with no bedclothes on it.

"Good morning, Ross." She hugged him from behind. "You really need to go back today?"

"If I want the Chattahoochee job, I do." He turned in her arms. "But I made an airline reservation for Thanksgiving to St. Louis as well, so I can meet your family. Then we can get married whenever we like."

"I like that. So, I'll see you in four weeks." Dorie hugged him as tightly as she could.

Ross picked her up and sat her on the futon. Sliding down beside her, he put one arm around her and clasped her hand with the other. "I will be fine in California. I need to learn how to fight the fires as much as I need to know how to replant afterward. I'm more concerned with the crazy stuff that's going on here."

"Mom said, 'Take the job in a small town. It'll be safer and friendlier.' Boy, was she wrong." Dorie snuggled up to Ross. "Coffee? Breakfast?"

"Let's go down to Java Joint after we fix our cup for the road. I need to see to your computer. When you're in Atlanta, you should pick up a new laptop." Ross kissed her.

Dorie extricated herself from his cozy protection. "I'll fix the coffee to go. You get all your things together."

She giggled, avoiding his grasp before he could pull her back onto the couch, then headed for the coffee machine. Dorie heard Ross whistle for Star to go out. The greyhound thundered down the stairs and rushed to go outside with Ross. She smiled. Some things were still good in the light of day.

***

Riley had spent yet another night in the bunks at the police station. Today he'd move into the townhouse until he could rebuild. The mattress set and frame he'd bought would be delivered today. All he'd need were sheets, blankets, pillows, and towels. So much work to replace what one accumulated over time. Replacing everything would cost a fortune. Good thing he had insurance. It was good to be back in uniform at least.

"Captain? How are you?" Joe Hardeman placed a cup of coffee on his desk. "Can I get you anything else?"

"I wouldn't say no to a doughnut or an omelet. That's not your job though, Joe." Riley sipped the espresso. "But if you don't mind, I wouldn't say no."

"I'll run down to Java Joint and get you something, then."

"Wait. Here's some cash. Can't have you paying for my breakfast, too."

"Thanks, Cap." Joe headed off on his errand. "I'll be right back."

Riley finished his notes for the morning briefing then gathered his courage and headed for the squad room. How could he explain what to do about his brother?

He joined the patrolmen and took the podium. Once the crowd settled, he tapped the lectern. "I don't know how to keep on working on this case. Ryker Johnson is still on the prowl. He turned up in Helen last night at Ross's house. Ross is heading for California this afternoon. Dorie must be safe while this man is on the loose. The sooner we catch him the sooner everyone is safer."

Patrolman Johnny Martin stood. "How do we tell you apart? I've seen the man. Up close it's easy to tell. From a distance, it could be you, Captain."

"Joe Hardeman has a code with me if it comes to it." Riley sighed. "This is difficult for me. Report anything you see that's unusual."

"Cap, you're back in uniform. That's unusual." The voice was unknown. The laughter broke throughout.

"Ha, ha, ha. Everyone's a comic. Remember that any old uniforms of mine were either burned in the fire or stolen in the burglary by Ryker Johnson." Riley leaned on the lectern. "This is serious business. My friends and our community are in danger from this madman. Let's get him.'"

Patrolmen shuffled out of the squad room accompanied by scraping chairs and casual talk. A few officers patted Riley on the back or nodded. He hated that this had become so personal. It was much harder to be objective, especially when he and his friends were in danger.

"Captain, Gemini?" Joe put his hand on Riley's shoulder.

"Conspiracy. Thanks Joe." Riley smiled. "Good to know I can be known."

"No problem, Captain. Have a great day."

Riley headed back to his office. Just as he sank into his chair, the phone rang.

"Captain McDonough."

"Hey, Riley, I'm at Java Joint. Want to come over? I'm headed for California this afternoon."

"Great. I'll be there in just a bit."

***

Dorie leaned over the last of the negatives. That's when she saw it. *Praise God!* The picture was a very young Mama Mary proudly holding two babies. Her father and an unknown young man were beside her. The next strip showed two babies, side by side, in a colorful nursery. The next showed Mama Mary holding one child and her father holding the other. Both boys came home from the hospital. The nursery was ready for two babies. Who was the young man? The father? What had happened to him?

The final photo on the strip was of one child in that nursery, presumably Riley. The second crib was gone. What had happened to Ryker?

"Find anything?" Greg startled her yet again.

"Something, but it doesn't explain it. Print these, please. I'd best put these photos in some kind of order, then give it over to Riley and his detectives to interpret."

Dorie stood and stretched. She would not miss crouching over this lightbox. She flipped off the lights and pulled the dust cover on it. With any luck, she'd never need it again. She packed up the organized strips in the box to take to Riley's new place later.

Back at her desk, Dorie unpacked the baby album and other photo albums she'd bought for Riley's family pictures. She spent the rest of the morning organizing the photos.

Dorie looked up as her broad-shouldered, red-bearded, sandy-haired man walked into the offices. She jumped up to greet him. He picked her up and kissed her in front of everyone in the newsroom. She felt the embarrassment climb into her cheeks, but just now, Dorie didn't care. He was hers, and she had a right to claim him.

"Ugh! PDAs in the newsroom!" It was Greg. "Never mind! They're already engaged. It doesn't count as an employee faux pas." The flash from his camera lit up the entire area. "Front page, Mr. Andrews. Daring crime-fighting investigative duo. Saving Daelin from murderers."

"Enough, Greg. Ross, put her down. This is her workplace, y'know." Mr. Andrews banished everybody back to their desks and work. He stuck out his hand to Ross. "Hear you're heading back to the West Coast today."

Ross put Dorie down and shook Mr. Andrews's

hand. "Yes, sir. I'll be taking Dorie with me to Atlanta shortly, so she can drive the car back."

"Be safe. We'll do our best to keep Dorie safe, too."

Ross nodded, the usual man of few words. Then he held up a flash drive.

"Is it? All of it?" Dorie nearly cried and shouted at the same time. A strange sounding shriek escaped.

"Jared says he got it all, but the computer is DOA." He teased her with it, holding it higher than she could reach easily. "What? You want this?"

Dorie put her hands on her hips. "Yes. Please give it to me, Ross."

"What's on here that's so important? You've got paper notes."

"Please don't mess with me about this!" She reached out to him and tickled him.

"No fair!" Ross clenched into a ball and handed her the flash drive. "No tickling! That's against the rules."

"I didn't know there were rules for that game you're playing." Dorie held up the flash drive then pouted. "Don't you have anything to do before you leave town? I have work to do."

The newsroom erupted in applause. Ross's face turned scarlet.

"Forgot we had an audience. I'll pick you up for lunch in an hour." He whispered into her ear, "I love you, Dorie," and kissed her. Then he beat a hasty retreat.

Dorie plugged the flash drive into a desktop computer she rarely used. All her data appeared to be there and accessible. She copied it onto the desktop then attached the flash drive to her press lanyard. Now all she needed was a new laptop. Lucky she'd be in Atlanta anyway today. Dorie sighed.

"You okay?" Greg was standing at the side of her desk. "I have these photos for you."

"Just a lot going on. That's all. Thanks for your help with all of this."

Greg smiled a dopey smile. "Loved working with you, Dorie. If you and Ross don't work out …"

"I'll keep it in mind." Dorie rolled her eyes at him once he headed back to his photo lab.

She looked at the photos Greg had given her. "Who is their father? Why did Ryker end up in foster care? Why did Mama Mary never tell Riley about him?" It seemed none of the important questions had answers.

Chapter 24

Chasing the truth …

Dorie sat in the chair across from Riley's cushy chair and checked her watch. She texted Ross. "At Daelin PD. Pick me up there."

Finally, Riley entered the room and plopped into the chair. "Sorry to keep you waiting. What can I do for you?"

"I thought you'd like to see these four photos."

Dorie placed them on the desk in the order of the film strip: Mama Mary with twins, Mama Mary with twins, her dad, and the strange man, twins in twin cribs in the nursery, then only one baby in the nursery.

Riley stood and stared at the photos. He picked up the one with the strange man. "Who's this? He looks familiar."

"If I was guessing, your father. But I don't know. I haven't found anything to suggest who your father is."

He picked up the last two photos. "Ryker came home from the hospital with me. What happened to him?"

"Not sure. I was about to see nursery records when Ryker burst in on me at the hospital. I do know Ryker was readmitted to the hospital shortly after you went home."

Riley puzzled. "Is this the last photo of him?"

Dorie reached into her backpack and pulled out another photo. "No, I found this picture of your Academy Graduation. Look at this man on the wall." She indicated a man at the edge of the stage. "Isn't that Ryker?"

"Let me see that." Riley took the photo and stared at it. He sat back down in his chair. "I never even knew he existed. He knew about me. Why didn't he say something to me? He was three feet away from me when I walked off that stage."

"I bet your mom took this photo. Do you think she ever noticed him in it?"

"Probably not if she thought he was dead. Someone made sure she only had one son to raise. Grandpa? Our father?" Riley swung side to side in the swivel chair while he thought. "After you've gone to Atlanta with Ross, see if you can get a look at those records."

"Well, speak of the devil."

Ross appeared so suddenly, Dorie nearly shrieked. "You scared me half to death."

"Why? Is something inappropriate going on here?" He waggled his eyebrows at her.

She burst into giggles.

"Have you seen these?" Riley handed Ross the photos.

Dorie tried to get control of her laughter while Ross flipped through the photos. *He's such a good man.*

"This man with your mom, I think he used to hang

out around us kids." Ross pointed to the strange man. "I'm sure I've seen him before. Didn't he coach our Little League team? Wasn't his name Lee … Lee … Kerr?"

"My goodness! You're named for him: Ri-Lee and Ry-Kerr!" Dorie nearly fell out of her chair. "I can google him or find him using facial recognition."

"No, Dorie, that would be the job of the police. Go have lunch, buy a computer, and send Ross back to California. We can meet up at Java Joint when you get back into Daelin. I'll know something by then."

"Setting up dates before I'm even gone." Ross sulked. "You should have the self-respect to wait until I'm out of the room. Or out of the state?"

Dorie stood and wrapped her arms around his waist. "Darling, there's only one man for me. Don't worry."

"Go before I feel the need to take insulin from all this sugar goin' on."

Ross stuck out his hand across the desk. "Take care of her for me. Just not too good."

Riley clasped his hand. "You got it. Take care of yourself as well."

***

After his friends left hand-in-hand, Riley took the photo of Lee Kerr to his computer whiz, Jack.

"Got a job for you, Jack. See if you can identify and find this man." Riley showed him the photo. "This man. Ross has tentatively identified him as Lee Kerr. Check the DNA matching banks for a similarity with my DNA and Ryker Johnson's DNA. I want to know if he's still alive and where he is."

"You thinking this guy's your dad?"

"Not sure, but I want to know everything as soon as possible." Riley headed for dispatch.

He swung into the communications nerve center. The room was darkened, illuminated by computer screens, and filled with dispatchers calmly taking 911 calls and sending appropriate emergency services to needy citizens.

"June, I want to post an all-points bulletin for a man named Lee Kerr."

The dark-haired older woman swiveled to give her attention to Riley. "Sho nuff, Cap McDonough. Give me more info."

"I'll have more info shortly. Go ahead and broadcast the APB in case someone knows him and knows where he lives." Riley tapped on her desk as she wrote out the memo for him to sign. When she finished the details, he scribbled his signature. "Thanks. Get it out immediately."

Riley strode to the desk sergeant. "Stevens, I am going out to the junk yard stakeout site if anyone needs me. If either of our APBs are responded to, I want to know immediately."

"Yes, sir, Captain." Sgt. Stevens saluted.

Riley nodded and grabbed his new uniform coat from the coat rack. All his uniforms had to be replaced. All his furniture. All his clothes and shoes. The list went on and on. Ryker had taken his home, his belongings, and his mother. He'd stolen and wrecked Dr. Eminem's purple car. He'd make sure the man couldn't hurt anyone else.

***

Dorie and Ross had picked up a new laptop at a big box store on the outskirts of Atlanta, had lunch, then hopped on the highway heading south through Atlanta toward the airport. Plenty of time. Until the highway traffic stopped. A bad accident up ahead had miles of traffic stationary. Between the semis, trucks, vans, and SUVs, no one could see anything.

"You're going to miss your flight." Dorie pounded on the steering wheel. "We should have gone straight to the airport instead of making all the side trips."

Ross took her hand and pressed it to his lips. "Maybe it's for the best."

"What about the Chattahoochee forest service job? What about our future together?" Dorie willed her tears to not spill down her cheeks. "This is about your dream coming true."

"You and Riley are in danger. I can't understand why I thought I could just fly off into the sunset leaving the two of you." He kissed her hand again. "I'll just call and explain the situation. I'm not the only person out there hoping to land a job by planting saplings."

They were stuck on an outer lane. People were maneuvering their cars to try to reach an exit. Dorie was just stuck. She wanted him to be happy. She didn't want him to sacrifice everything for her. Then if things didn't work out, he'd blame her.

"Hey, sweetheart. It's really okay. I'd never forgive myself if something happened to you or Riley. What kind of future would I have then?" His voice was as tender as his touch.

His phone rang.

"Hello? … Yes, it's Ross MacAvoy." He nodded his head, as though they could see or hear that. "Well, we're stuck in Atlanta traffic. … I'm not going to make the flight. … You may as well cancel the airline tickets and get your money back. … Yeah, the hotel room too. … We're having a crisis. I need to be here to help. … It involves my fiancée and my best friend. … We'll talk Monday then."

Dorie reached over and grasped his hand. "I can't believe you just quit your job over horrific traffic."

"I can't believe you'd expect me to just leave you." Ross leaned over to her and kissed her. "I need to be here for you. Let's go home."

Ross pointed out a paved U-turn between the highway sections that clearly stated, "No U-Turns." Traffic inched closer toward the median crossover.

"Are you sure we should?" Dorie worried about things like crossing the median without permission.

As she watched, several cars used the median crossover to get to the uncongested highway.

"I think, any port in the storm, my love." Ross kissed her hand. "Let's go home."

"Okay, but if I get pulled over and get a ticket, Riley owes me a big favor." Dorie reached the crossover and made the illegal U-turn to get back to Riley.

Ross threw back his head and laughed.

Chapter 25

Visiting the campsite …

The sun slowly set to the west of the dump as Riley entered. He turned on the fog lights on the Chief's SUV to avoid being wholly conspicuous as he approached the stakeout team. He hid his SUV behind a stack of rusting vehicles, shut down the engine and cut the lights. Then he joined the officers in their car, climbing into the back seat.

"Any sign of my brother?"

"No, sir. Maybe he's left the area." Officer Joe Hardeman took a slurp of his coffee. "Doughnut, Cap?

"No, thank you." Riley peered at the scrapheap that was his brother's hideaway. No heat, no electricity, no friends, no family except for him. And he was out to arrest and convict his own brother. Riley knew God wanted him to forgive Ryker and find a way to love him. *But God, he murdered our mother and my dog, burned two houses to the ground, and threatened my friends. How can I forgive him?*

"Okay, new plan. I'm going to wait for Ryker in his place. He still has valuables there."

Joe nearly choked on his coffee. "Cap, that's a

terrible idea. He could kill you before we could draw our weapons."

"Then I suggest you be ready." Riley climbed out of the backseat and gently closed the door. He picked his way through the scrap and rusting metal until he reached the cave-like entrance to his brother's hideout. Cans of beans and Vienna sausages were tossed in one corner with molding bread and cases of soda. The large can for a stove was cold. Riley's baby book sat on an overturned box. A crate seemed to serve as a chair.

Riley ignited the fuel in the can and fed it with the paper and sticks nearby. Nearly Halloween. The weather had turned chilly, as it should when approaching winter. This manhunt had to end, for everyone's sake. Riley picked up the baby book. Under it was a well-worn Bible with markers throughout. The cover page was inscribed to "Ryker Johnson" with a date that indicated it was the day he became a Christian. He opened it to the New Testament markers.

Matthew 5:21-22 was underlined. *You have heard that it was said to the people long ago, 'You shall not murder, and anyone who murders will be subject to judgment.' But I tell you that anyone who is angry with a brother or sister will be subject to judgment. Again, anyone who says to a brother or sister, 'Raca,' is answerable to the court. And anyone who says, 'You fool!' will be in danger of the fire of hell.*

In the margin of the underlined verses was scrawled, "RILEY". How long had Ryker known he had a brother, much less a twin?

The next marker was at an underlined James 4:2.

You crave what you do not have. You kill and covet, but are unable to obtain it. You quarrel and fight. You do not have, because you do not ask. Next to the verse was scrawled "FAMILY".

The third marker was at <u>1 John 2:9</u>, 11. *If anyone claims to be in the light but hates his brother, he is still in the darkness. ... But whoever hates his brother is in the darkness and walks in the darkness. He does not know where he is going, because the darkness has blinded his eyes.*

Again, Riley saw his name in the margin. Did Ryker struggle with his hatred of his brother versus his own Christianity?

The fourth marker was at 1 John 3:15. *Anyone who hates a brother or sister is a murderer, and you know that no murderer has eternal life residing in him.* Did he have no hope then of heaven? Why not murder then? His brother needed forgiveness more than punishment. He needed hope. Perhaps he could do that. Or could he?

Riley took a business card from his jacket and scribbled a note, "If you are a Christian, God can forgive even murder. If you are not a Christian, refusing Christ is the only unforgivable sin. See 1 John 1:9." He wrote "RYKER" on the end. Then he underlined the verse, *If we confess our sins, he is faithful and just and will forgive us our sins and purify us from all unrighteousness.* Then Riley stuck the card in the Bible, so that "RYKER" stuck out.

He heard a rustle in the distance. The hair on the back of his neck stirred, but was it wariness or just a cold breeze? He stood and tried to see into the darkness. That's when the patrol car flashed its lights at him. He carefully picked his way through the rusting metal toward the surveillance team.

"What's up?"

"Your APB on Lee Kerr has several call-ins. Thought you'd like to come in and review the leads."

Riley rubbed his stubbly chin. "Okay, but I need an immediate call if Ryker comes back here."

"You got it, Captain." Joe handed him a doughnut in a napkin. "For the road."

"Thanks." Riley nodded, took the doughnut, then headed back to Daelin PD.

***

Ross and Dorie pulled up outside Riley's new townhouse, just a few doors from where Ross had lived. The place was dark, so Ross phoned him on speakerphone so Dorie could hear.

When Riley answered, Ross started the conversation. "Riley, we're outside your place. We brought pizza. Where are you?"

"Rolling into the parking lot at Daelin PD. Aren't you supposed to be on a plane to California?"

Ross laughed. "Yep. Decided not to go. I'm needed here."

"You can do that?"

"Well, I did it. What repercussions there might be are yet to be seen." Ross raised his eyebrows, and Dorie laughed.

"I have some responses to my APB on Lee Kerr, so I'll see what I've got. Then I'll be home." Riley slammed the door of the SUV and the beep said he'd locked it. "Let yourself in. The key is under the mat. I know, I know, not very secure. But I have friends that come unannounced."

Dorie jumped out and found the key.

"Dorie's got the key, so we'll put the pizza in the oven to stay warm. We'll set up Dorie's new laptop while we wait."

"The WI-FI password is on the modem. Again, not very secure, I know."

Dorie opened the door and pulled the computer box into the townhouse. Ross came in after her. She set up the computer, then connected to the WI-FI.

Ross fixed them each a cup of coffee. He searched in the refrigerator and the pantry for a snack while they waited on Riley and the pizza. He found a bag of chocolate chip cookies.

"Coffee. Perfect, sweetheart. Cookies are wonderful. Thank you."

Ross snuggled up beside her on the new sofa with boxes for a coffee table.

Dorie inserted the flash drive into the new computer and uploaded the data.

"All there?" Ross peeked over her.

"Looks like. Thank you so much." Dorie kissed him, then turned and hugged him. "You have saved my career."

"Not my first goal. Can't stand having you unhappy, though." Ross wrapped his arm around her. "Wonder when Riley will finally be here. I'm hungry."

"On the other hand, we have the place to ourselves." Dorie took his hand.

"True, but we could be at our own house … making sure we're not too comfortable together." Ross twisted his mouth. "I'm home now. What will we do?"

"Should I move out? After all, it is your house."

"No, darling. I would not evict you from our future bedroom. This townhouse probably has a second bedroom. Perhaps I can stay here until after Thanksgiving."

"Do you think I'm making too big a deal about meeting my family?" Dorie sank into his hug. "Don't you have any family?"

Ross sighed. *No way could he tell her the whole truth about his family. But he couldn't not tell her about his mom.* "Dorie, I have no family to have an opinion about who I marry. I'll tell you more later."

Dorie gave him a quizzical look. Fortunately, she didn't ask any more questions. *Hard to tell the truth about such a thing.*

The door opened, and Riley burst in.

"Glad to see you making yourself at home. Thought there was a pizza on the premises."

Dorie hopped up from the sofa and headed for the kitchen.

"What did you find out about Lee Kerr?"

"Seems he's in Atlanta. We'll find him tomorrow."

Chapter 26

Facing down a twin …

Riley watched Dorie and Ross drive away. He picked up the paper plates and dirty cups and took them to the kitchen.

"So now it's just us, brother." Ryker sat on the counter with a gun pointed at Riley.

"How did you get in?"

"Same way your friend's girl got in. Old trick. Not too secure though."

Riley propped himself against the sink. "You've been here the whole time?"

"I'm here to see you, not your friends." Ryker tapped the gun on his leg.

Riley crossed his arms. "I went to your hideaway at the dump and left you a message. You never came."

"How can I with your stooges watchin' the place all the time?" Ryker hopped down off the counter. "Let's go sit on the couch. May as well be comfortable while we're making our acquaintance."

"Sure, come sit down. I'm still trying to replace my furniture from the fire." Riley moved smoothly toward the living room. "You have no need for a gun here. My gun is in the gun safe. No one's coming."

Ryker perched on the makeshift coffee table. "I watched you lock it away. I was in the closet, before your friends arrived. I heard it all, your grand plans. But this, this is between us."

"You killed our mom. She didn't know. She thought you were dead. That's why you weren't known, looked for, expected …"

Ryker pistol-whipped him. "You have no right. I am a person. I am not dead. She had to know I was alive. She was my mom. Same as you. I have the right to be mad."

Riley touched his face and brought down blood from the wound. "Ryker, you do have a right to be mad. You do not have the right to burn down houses nor to kill people."

Ryker hit him again. "You don't understand. I was alone. I thought I was alone. Then I found out I had family. But they didn't want me!"

His voice rattled in the mostly empty townhouse. Riley wanted to calm him. He had to convince him to give himself up to him. He couldn't allow Ryker loose in the community. What could he say?

"My friend Dorie has been going through Mama's photos in order to reproduce the albums you took. She found pictures of you." Riley carefully, slowly, reached into his pocket for the pictures she'd brought him.

"Is that so?" Ryker placed the gun into his lap.

"I'm also supposed to have guys come from Atlanta with the man who could be our dad. I've got an APB out on a man named Lee Kerr." He put the pictures on the space beside Ryker. "Get it? Ri-Lee and Ri-ker."

"I'm not stupid." Ryker picked up the pictures. "Who's the other man?"

"Grandpa. Mama's dad." Riley watched Ryker to see if he'd relax. "See, we both came home to the nursery Mama created for us. The pictures show she was proud of us both. I don't know what happened, Ryker. Notice the last picture shows only me. Don't you think I noticed you missing?"

"You were a baby. What did you know?" Ryker put the pictures down. "So, this is when I ended up in foster care, and you got to stay. What made you better?"

"Nothing. Nothing made me better. We're identical, you and me. Anyone can see that." Riley's mind ran as fast as it could thinking of redeeming ways to encourage Ryker. And reduce his anger. "Dorie was working on the why when you trashed her laptop. It put her work back a couple days."

Ryker picked up the gun again and threatened Riley with it. "She was there but didn't answer me. It made me angry."

"I get that. Women are sometimes difficult to understand." Riley laughed a little. "She was trying to help and was afraid."

"So, who's this Ross guy she's engaged to? How come he's 'like your brother'?"

Riley forced himself to lean back on the couch. "He was the brother I didn't have. Proof I missed you, don't you think?"

Ryker stood. "Don't patronize me. You replaced me with a substitute."

Riley's phone rang. He reached for it. Ryker grabbed it and threw it across the room.

"You don't need to talk to nobody right now but me."

"People need to coordinate with me. If they can't, they will start looking for me." Riley tried to keep his voice even and controlled. "Why not let me call them back?"

Ryker smirked. "No, I don't think so, Big Chief of Police. Imagine being someone no one wants to talk to for a few hours." Ryker grabbed Riley's arm and pulled him out of the couch. "Let's go. Leave the phone here."

***

Dorie hurried into Ross's house and plopped on the futon. She popped up the new laptop and read through the data she had uploaded from the flash drive. Star came up and nuzzled her hand as she tried to type.

"Stop, Star, I can't work like that." Dorie laughed. She finally stopped trying and grabbed Star's long-nosed face and rubbed her velvety fur. "I love you." She buried her face in the dog's fur.

Ross struggled in the front door with his luggage and takeout bags. "Sure, the dog did nothing today, but she gets affection. Me, nada."

"Jealous? Of a girl dog?" Dorie patted the dog, then stood to rescue the takeout. "You will get your fair share of affection, my love." She put her arms around his neck. "Why do you look so sad?"

"I tried Riley." Ross leaned down and kissed her. "He didn't answer. What if Ryker got to him? I should have stayed with him."

"Maybe. But he is the Chief of Police. He has many officers concerned for his safety. He should be fine."

Ross tilted his head with a puzzled face. "Maybe. I think I'll call it in to PD anyway." He turned and walked back out with his phone.

Dorie could hear him. He sounded very concerned. Perhaps they should have stayed with Riley or insisted he come back to Helen with them. She sat back down at the computer and googled 'Ryker McDonough, public records', something she should have done ages ago.

"Birth certificate, death certificate?" Dorie clicked on the death certificate. "Ryker Jonah McDonough, born May 28, 1990, died June 7, 1990. Cause of death: Jaundice, liver failure."

Dorie sorted through her notes. "Admitted June 6, 1990. Died June 7, 1990?" What was this about? A way to get rid of one of the twins?

Chapter 27

Saving the Captain …

Ross rushed into the house. "Something's happened in Daelin. No one can get hold of Riley. He's not at home. His phone is at his place. There's also blood on the new couch."

"Where are you going?" Dorie grabbed Ross's arm as he headed for the door. "I'm going too."

"No, stay here." Ross took her hand and kissed it. "Riley may come here if he is on the run from Ryker. Lock the doors. Be here, in case he needs a safe place to come to. Police detail is still here." He kissed her then headed out the door. "Call me if he does come here."

Dorie watched him from the door. He spoke to the police detail in the front yard, then climbed in the old truck. Ross revved the old engine, threw it in gear, and headed down the mountain. She closed the door and bolted it. She went from window to window and to the deck door.

When she reached the door to the garage, it was unlocked. Dorie opened the door and stared out into the empty garage. It looked fine, but the attic light was on. She crept to the stairway, picked up a heavy plank of flooring, then turned off the light. She expected someone to come scrambling from the attic. Dorie heard nothing.

Back in the house, Dorie locked the door to the garage from the house but wondered who had been in the attic with the light on. She and Ross had been gone all day. A shiver had her reaching for his ratty sweater he kept on the back of the futon. She went back to her computer, turning on all the lights on the way back.

***

Riley and Ryker pulled up to a storage unit place. Ryker handed him the key while he kept the gun trained on Riley's back.

"Open G-4." Ryker's voice was rough and husky. No doubt about it. His life had been hard. And he carried the physical scars as well as the emotional ones.

Riley peered at the labels of the units. The security lights hummed their discordant song while he searched.

"Over there!" Ryker pushed him toward the G-4 unit. "Whatta ya waitin' for? Open it up."

Riley inserted and turned the key. He reached down for the handle but let it hit him in the face where he'd already bled tonight. He made sure a good smear was around the handle.

"You are so clumsy. I can't believe you graduated from the Police Academy except I was there to see it. I was proud of you then." Ryker shoved Riley into the unit and brought the door back down as he turned on the overhead light. He also turned on a space heater. "Now this here's a palace compared to the dump. Sit." He motioned with the gun toward a barrel near the heater.

"Nice digs. Food and everything. Even a microwave." Riley was finding it hard to stay alert yet calm. "You got any popcorn for the microwave?"

"Of course. This here's class digs. Don't you try anything and maybe we can be pals." Ryker edged over to the stack of food and pulled out a cellophane wrapped bag of popcorn. He unwrapped it, slammed it into the microwave, and pushed the appropriate button.

The poppity-pop soothed Riley's nerves some. The smell would be hard to miss if anyone came looking for him. The ding startled him, nonetheless.

"Here ya go, bro." Ryker handed the bag to him by the steaming hot edge. "Here's a bowl to dump it in. Ya gotta eat it while it's hot, after all."

The bowl wasn't exactly clean, but it wasn't unusable either. Riley opened the bag and dumped the contents. He offered some to Ryker who took a buttery handful.

"Now that's the ticket on a cold night. If only we had a fire." Ryker laughed. "Guess you've had enough of that though."

Riley nodded. "You got that right. I don't want to clean up any more ashes. Can I have one of those Cokes?"

"You bet." Ryker handed him a cold can. "So why do you suppose they kept you and not me?"

"Who can tell?" Riley took a deep sip of the soda. "Dorie said you were taken back to the hospital shortly after our birth. She didn't have time to find out why."

"This Dorie chick is handy to have around, isn't

she? Don't you do any policework?"

Riley nodded. "She's a great investigator. Maybe I should hire her away from the *Beacon,* whatcha think?"

"You're in love with her." Ryker chuckled. "She's cute, but doesn't she belong to Ross?"

"Yes. She's not my girl." Riley washed back some popcorn. "Ross got there first. They're good together. I don't mind."

"That's a lie." Ryker stepped closer. "Your face turns red when you lie. I guess you'd better tell me the truth if I know your tell."

"You're right. It does bother me, especially when he flew off to California, leaving me to take care of her." Riley munched another handful of popcorn. "We're good friends though."

"'Cause you're such a good guy, white hat and all." Ryker laid down the gun. "I'm gonna let you take me in. I just wanted to get to know you, see if you were the real deal. You are."

Riley heard the sounds he'd hoped to hear: the crunch of heavy-duty tires on the gravel parking lot, feet jumping down into the site, the sound of rifles being locked and loaded. Operational tactical team, heroes for hire. Now it was his turn to save his brother. "Do you hear what I'm hearing?"

"Yep, my time is coming to an end, I suppose. For the record, I never wanted to kill our mom. She said she loved me still, even after I hit her. I flew into a rage. She literally could have said anything else, and I would have walked away. How could she love me when she didn't even know me?" Ryker handed the gun to Riley. "Just like, how can God love me after all the bad I've done?"

"Forgiveness, Ryker. Because there's forgiveness." Riley stood and put the gun in his waistband. "Come on, let's leave here for a more comfortable building."

Spotlights blinded them as Ryker raised the garage-type door. Ryker put his hands in the air.

Riley called out. "It's okay. He's surrendered to me."

A uniformed amoeba swarmed around them and took Ryker into custody. Riley handed the gun to Officer Joe Hardeman.

"Gemini?"

"Conspiracy, Joe. And it's over." Riley slapped Joe on the back and joined his men in celebration.

***

Ross pulled up to the station as the procession of vehicles was also pulling into the lot.

Riley stepped out of the Captain's SUV and stretched.

"Riley!" Ross hurried across the lot to enwrap him in a manly bear hug. "They told me they couldn't locate you when you didn't answer your phone. What happened to your face?"

Riley clapped him on the back. "My brother was in the townhouse while we were there. After you left, we took some time to get acquainted."

"Is that code for he abducted you?" Ross noticed a squad car pull up and open the backseat door. A man who had to be Ryker was helped out of the car. "Did he hit you?"

"Did he abduct and assault me? Is that what you think I should charge him with?" Riley's voice held a quiver. "After two counts of arson, assault and murder of my mom, and grand theft auto, what happened to me was nothing."

"Aren't you going to hold him responsible?" Ross heard the anger in his own voice. *How could he let the guy off? Brother or no, he was on the hook for some serious crimes.* "What about the assault on Angela and menacing Dorie with a gun and destroying her laptop?" Fatigue seemed to overwhelm him. This man had terrorized Daelin, and Riley was going to write off part of it.

Riley clapped him on the back. "Don't worry. He'll be in jail a very long time. Let's have some coffee. I got one of those fancy coffee machines for the station. Haven't even opened it. You can teach me how to use it."

Chapter 28

Finding the truth …

Ross tiptoed into the house in Helen. Every light had to be burning. He walked through as quietly as possible, turning off each light switch. The deck lights were even on. *What had gone on here after I left?*

He found Dorie fast asleep on the couch, snuggled in one of his old sweaters. A plank of flooring lay beside her on the floor. He carefully slid in beside her. No way did he want her to startle awake and hit him with that board. She stirred, and he pulled her into his lap.

"Good morning. What happened here last night?" Ross kissed her forehead.

Dorie was suddenly alert. "The light was on in the attic."

"No one was in the attic yesterday. Why would the light be on?" Ross was edgy. Who would have been in the attic if not one of them?

"You tell me. While you were in California, I thought I heard someone up there, walking around, rummaging through the stuff." She sounded terrified, which accounted for every light being on. "Who else would have a key to the garage?"

"Absolutely no one. I swear it. When Grandpa passed, I was the only person left with a key." Ross felt a doubt creep into his mind. *No, it couldn't be. She's still locked up, wasn't she?*

He could see in her eyes that Dorie didn't believe him. Maybe he didn't believe himself either.

"Ok, then. I need a cup of coffee. One for you?" Dorie jumped up from Ross's lap.

"No, I've been helping Riley try out his fancy coffee machine all night. I think I need some sleep, if that's okay with you." Ross explained what had happened with Riley and Ryker.

"What's going to happen with Ryker?" Dorie started the machine to clicking, whirring, and steaming.

"I have a feeling he's going to plead guilty to whatever they end up charging him with." Ross yawned. Caffeine was not going to keep him awake much longer. "I'm going to stretch out on the futon. Kiss me before you leave for work."

***

Dorie dressed and gathered her notes and new laptop. Ross was sound asleep. Star lay beside him on the floor. She looked up as Dorie came over to kiss Ross good-bye.

"Take good care of him, Star. I'll be back later."

Star snorted and laid her head back on the floor. Dorie kissed Ross carefully, then headed for Daelin.

First, she'd go to the station to check in with Riley and let him know what she'd found out about Ryker's death certificate. She also wanted to be there when Lee Kerr arrived from Atlanta. Then she needed to finish writing the article about Ryker's arrest. It would be a busy day.

As Dorie pulled into Daelin PD, another car pulled in next to her. The car had the emblem of an eagle and the words "City of Atlanta Police". The man in the back seat looked amazingly like Riley. He must be Lee Kerr. Not much doubt about it. She hopped out of her car.

"Good morning, officers." She ran around the car to where the man was being escorted out of the back seat. "I'm Dorie Hudson, friend of Riley McDonough. I'm also Ross MacAvoy's fiancée. Is this Lee Kerr? I understand he was an important person in their younger lives."

"Fiancée of Ross MacAvoy? And friend of Riley McDonough? How are those guys? They must be nearly thirty by now. They were inseparable as kids."

"Ma'am, I need to escort Mr. Kerr into the station." The officer was big, brawny, and scary. "If Captain McDonough allows it, you can speak with Mr. Kerr after we conclude the business at hand."

"One more question?" Dorie pushed on though the paper in her hand quivered. "Do you know what happened to Ryker McDonough?"

"I have no comment on that subject." Lee Kerr turned from her and allowed himself to be hurried into Daelin PD.

Dorie followed them in.

"Hey, Dorie!" Sgt. Stevens waved from his desk sergeant post. "Go on back. Captain's in his office, and doughnuts are in the break room."

Dorie headed back to Riley's office, lifting her eyebrows as she passed the contingent from Atlanta.

She found him with his head in his hands and his elbows propped on the desk. He looked up as she sat down.

"Good morning. I can barely keep my eyes open." Riley looked up. "What's up?"

"Your dad is here from Atlanta."

Riley was suddenly alert. "Lee Kerr is here?" His desk phone began ringing. "Yes? Send him back to Interrogation 1." He looked at Dorie. "Want to watch on the other side of the mirror?"

"Yes. Privileged information or public?"

Riley shook his head. "Don't know until I hear what he says. Take notes, no recording. I'll meet with you afterwards to determine if what he said is public knowledge. Okay with you?"

Dorie nodded. It was like being able to buy the whole store of penny candy! She pulled a yellow legal pad and a pen from her backpack and stashed the bag under Riley's desk. Shouldn't a police station be safe enough to hide your purse/computer bag?

She followed Riley down the hall. He opened a door for her then entered the next door. Dorie saw him sit opposite Lee Kerr through the two-way mirror in the interrogation room. The Atlanta policemen stood at attention, each in a corner of the room.

"Lee Kerr. I know you, don't I?" Riley shuffled some papers. Dorie could see they were blank.

"I was around a lot when you were a kid. Coached your Little League baseball team for a while."

Riley stared him down. "I remember that. Were you also around for my birth?"

Lee looked at him, puzzling over his answer.

"Yes."

Riley pulled the photo with Lee Kerr in it. "What do you have to say about this photo?"

Lee took the photo and stared at it. "This picture was taken over thirty years ago. Where did you get this?"

"You are not under arrest nor are you under oath, but I warn you that you should tell me the truth at this juncture. I've had no sleep tonight due to the clues I have in this photo." Riley's voice strained. "Identify the people in this photo, please."

"Mr. McDonough, Mary McDonough, her twin boys you and Ryker, and yes, that's me." Lee laid the photo back on the table. "What of it?"

"I didn't know I had a twin brother until a couple weeks ago." Riley pounded the table making Lee wince. "What happened to Ryker?"

"He died." Lee was curt. "It was nobody's fault."

"Liar! He is not dead. He's in the cells here." Riley stood and leaned on the table. "Try again!"

"What do you want me to say? Why don't you ask your mother?"

Dorie cringed. Would Riley explode? She could see his leg pumping vigorously beside the chair.

Riley returned to his seat and shuffled his papers. "Mr. Kerr, my mother was murdered by my brother. She never shared that secret with me until her dying breath. I was hoping you could tell me since I'm guessing you're my father."

"Okay, yes, I'm your father. So, you figured out the code." Lee leaned back in his chair now that the secret was out. "You have Ryker here? Can I see him?"

"Why did you abandon us? You realize you owed her child support. Why did you give up Ryker to foster care?" Riley was out of his chair again and pacing the floor.

"I wasn't the one who wanted one of the twins out of the picture." Lee stabbed the picture with his finger. "Her dad was the one. So, he faked Ryker's death, changed his name, and put him into foster care. He wanted me gone, too."

"Why would you let him do that?" Riley had him by the collar. "Why weren't you around?"

"I wanted to marry her. He paid me off to leave Mary. Her dad didn't want me around, so he gave me money to go away."

Riley let go of him. "Grandpa removed you and Ryker from my life?"

"Think about it. I came back to coach Little League right after your grandpa died." Lee hung his head. "I never got the courage to see Mary. I figured she'd had enough heartache from me."

Riley picked up the photos and papers and left the interrogation room. Dorie hurried into the hall. He was slumped against the wall.

"Are you all right?" Dorie put her hand on his shoulder. "I thought you were going to hit him."

"What would that prove at this point?" He shrugged her hand off his shoulder. "I just need some time to think."

Dorie went out to the lobby of Daelin PD after retrieving her backpack from under Riley's desk. She got out her computer and started typing up the end of the story. So much deception and heartache! Where was the happy ever after? Where was God in all this mess? She typed up the story basics, then headed back to the *Beacon*.

Chapter 29

Searching for the good …

Riley plopped into his desk chair, picked up his phone, and called the evidence lock up.

"Sonny, do we have all the pertinent evidence for the Ryker Johnson case?"

"Yes, sir. All boxed and itemized."

Riley pressed. "I'd like the Bible. Go ahead and pull it for me. I'll be down shortly to sign for it."

"You got it, Cap. Give me ten minutes to get it and the paperwork."

Was it worth a try to talk some truth to Ryker? Guess he'd find out. Riley headed down to Evidence. Sonny Taylor was the Evidence clerk. He was a burly guy, riding out his time to retirement with full pension in a clerk's chair in a cage. How he hoped he'd never do that

"Sonny, have you got what I want?" Riley signed the logbook.

"Yes, sir. One gen-U-Ine leather Bible, owner one Ryker Johnson." He produced the Bible sealed in a plastic evidence bag. "I'll sign the seal, then you sign the seal before we break it."

They went through the prerequisite steps to preserve chain of custody. Riley flipped through the

Bible to the place he'd placed his business card. Ryker hadn't had time to go back to the site once the surveillance team was in place. Well, it was time Ryker had his Bible back.

Riley took the stairs to the basement where the cells were located. Lee Kerr was in one, charged with evading child support. Ryker was at the opposite end from their father.

"Riley, can't we just talk? I understand that you're angry with me, but I did try to be part of your life until your mom found out I was coaching that team." Lee held onto the bars. "At least let me explain."

"Not now, Mr. Kerr." Riley kept walking. He had a different purpose this morning.

When he reached Ryker's cell, he pulled a chair up outside the bars. "I've got something for you."

"What could you give me that matters?" Ryker lay curled in a ball in the back corner of the cell. "Why even bother? You haven't before now."

"I didn't even know you existed, Ryker. How could I …" It was the same argument and Riley was tired of it. "Anyway, here's your Bible. Tell me about it."

Ryker crept forward, like a monkey in a cage, fearful, suspicious, curious, and wanting the book. He finally got close enough to snatch it through the bars and out of Riley's hand. He stroked the cover then double checked the owner page.

"Tell me about this Bible. Who gave it to you and why? Was it a special occasion?"

Ryker sneered. "I don't want to talk to you."

Riley stood and shrugged. "Let the officer know when you do. I want to know you."

Ryker scrambled back to his corner with the Bible. Riley headed back to his office, turning for a last look as he left.

After lunch, the detainment officer phoned. Ryker wanted to talk. Riley hurried down to the cells.

"Heard you wanted to talk to me." Riley pulled up the chair and had a seat.

Ryker looked him in the eye. "You really want to know?

Riley nodded.

"My foster mom at the time took me to church with her. This date is when I was baptized after I made a profession of faith in Jesus Christ. But not long after that I discovered I had a twin and a mom who'd sent me to foster care. The rage filled me up to overflowing. I've done some terrible things. God can't forgive me now."

"Did you truly become a Christian back then?" Riley wasn't certain if the question would draw Ryker into conversation or send him back to his corner again.

"I saw the bookmark you left in my Bible. You really think it's as easy as asking for forgiveness?"

Riley thought for a minute. "Do you think the Bible is true?"

"Well, yeah, bro." Ryker shot him an annoyed look. "That's why I carried it with me all these years."

Riley nodded. "Then it doesn't matter what I think about it. If it's true, it's true no matter what I think."

Ryker pondered Riley's answer. He opened the Bible back to 1 John 1:9 and read it aloud. "If we confess our sins, he is faithful and just and will forgive us our sins and purify us from all unrighteousness."

"If you're His child, He never stops loving you nor forgiving you." Riley pulled the chair closer to the cell. "And you're my brother twice."

Ryker nodded. A tear ran down his cheek. Finally, he buried his head in his arms and wept. Riley put his hand through the bars and laid it on his shoulder. The officer on guard jumped to his feet and rushed toward him. Riley held up his other hand to stop the guard from interrupting them.

"It's okay, Ryker. I forgive you, too." Riley's heart hurt, but it was better to forgive him than to hold onto the bitterness. "Let me know if you need anything."

"It's okay, Ryker. I forgive you, too." Riley's heart hurt, but it was better to forgive him than to hold onto the bitterness. "Let me know if you need anything."

Riley walked past the row of empty cells until he reached Lee Kerr's.

"Okay, Mr. Kerr, what do you want to discuss?" Riley sighed. It was just too much to take in.

Mr. Kerr hurried to the bars near Riley. "I wanted to tell you about us, all of us."

The guard grabbed him a chair. There was no reason to move Mr. Kerr to interrogation. He and Ryker were the only ones with an interest in what he might have to say about the past. "So, spill it before I lose patience with you."

Mr. Kerr raised his hands palms forward as though fighting off an attacker. "I can understand that you're upset."

"Upset doesn't even cover what I'm feeling. Don't presume to know me, sir."

"Got it, got it. Okay, you probably want to know about me and Mary." He raised his eyebrows in a question.

Riley sat in the chair. "Ancient history. Mama's dead, Ryker's going prison for murder and other mayhem. None of us has ever married. Wonder why."

"That's fair. I wasn't there for any of you. But it wasn't because Mary and me didn't love each other. We did! And we were excited about you boys. But Mary's dad didn't like me and didn't want me around. That's why we never married." He licked his lips. "Can I get some water?"

The guard hurried off to get a bottle of water.

"Is it fair to slander my grandfather after he's already dead? And how can I check out your version of truth when Mama's dead too? Too little, too late." Riley shook his head. How would what he had to say change anything?

"Your grandfather is why Ryker was put in foster care."

Ryker spoke up from his cell. "Speak up if you're gonna tell tales on me."

"Fair enough, Ryker. I can't believe the three of us are together."

"A doggone family reunion, old man." Ryker's tone of derision cut through the cells.

Lee Kerr nodded. "Okay. Ryker got the jaundice real bad. He was turning yellow and everything. Mary was still recovering from giving birth and nursing, so Grandpa took little Ryker to the hospital. But when Mary went to see him the next day, he was gone. The hospital folks told her he'd died of the jaundice. We didn't know no different."

"So why blame my grandfather?" Riley felt anger rising in him. "What makes you think he had anything to do with it?"

"'Cause later, when Mary and me were talkin' about gettin' married and gettin' our own place, Mr. McDonough pulled me aside and told me he did it."

"Did what?" Ryker threw something across his cell. It clanged in the corner against the cement.

"Had you declared dead and placed in foster care under a different name."

Ryker swore.

Riley sighed. "And he could do that because…?"

"Don't you know he was Mayor of Daelin at the time?" Lee Kerr sat down on the cot in the cell. "He told me to stay away from Mary and my boys, or he'd find something to charge me with. He offered me a thousand dollars to stay away. So, I did. You may not remember it, but I came back and coached your ball team right after your grandpa died. You and Ross were just as tight as twins in those days."

"I knew it!" Ryker yelled from his cell. "Ross took my place."

"I'm done!" Riley stood and walked out of the holding area.

Riley walked back to his office and closed his door. He turned his chair around. Then he prayed and cried himself.

Chapter 30

Planning for the future …

The sun shone through the window into Dorie's face. Saturday. And the whole mess was over. Riley's brother was arrested and in jail. Riley was safe. She rolled over and stretched.

Crash! Something fell over her head in the attic.

Dorie jumped from the bed, threw on her robe, and ran to the garage and the attic steps. Star took up the chase and got there first. Then she began roo-ing, a shrill high-pitched howl unique to the greyhound breed.

"Stop, Star." Dorie climbed the steps, wondering where that plank of flooring was. She reached the top, opened the creaky door, and flipped on the light. Star rushed in before Dorie could stop her.

"Sorry!" Ross stood in the midst of a collapsed pile of boxes with Star dancing around him. "I didn't want to wake you. Good thing I hid that piece of flooring, huh?"

Dorie hugged herself and tried to settle the urge to scream. "You scared me near to death."

"You look beautiful?" Ross walked through the attic, avoiding all the piles of stuff from at least three generations. He wrapped her in his arms. "I just wanted to get an early start. We need furniture. It's hard to know what to buy without seeing what's usable up here." He kissed her. "Are you okay?"

"If I knew someone else was in the house, it would help when I hear strange sounds. Wake me up next time." Dorie struggled out of his grasp, trying to storm away. Ross caught her robe and pulled her back.

"But you do love me, right?"

"Yes." Dorie kissed him and headed back downstairs to avoid the temptation to stay.

After coffee and an inventory of the usable furniture in the attic, they went shopping.

***

Ross and Riley struggled with the new couch. Dorie put the pizza in the oven to keep it warm.

"This looks serious, Ross. New furniture means serious co-habitation happening. When's the wedding?"

"Not until after I meet the Hudson family Thanksgiving. Maybe not until Spring after I have a job."

Riley helped him get it into position. "Are you so anxious to give up your freedom?"

"I thought you understood how wonderful Dorie is. I live in fear that someone will come along and love her better than I can." Ross set the couch down. "I think freedom is marriage to Dorie. I won't ever have to worry once she's officially mine."

"Won't you?" Dorie appeared from nowhere. "You needn't worry about that. Don't you know how determined I am to be your wife?"

"You weren't supposed to hear that." Ross

plopped onto the couch. "I can't even imagine my life without you."

Riley plopped on the opposite end of the couch. "You two are too much! Just get married and get it over with."

"That's the plan." Dorie put her arms around Ross's neck from behind. "You needn't worry. Why not Christmas?"

"A small Christmas wedding?" Ross turned 'round and kissed her. "Sounds perfect."

"Perfect except we still got Halloween and Thanksgiving before then." Riley moaned as he fell over on the couch. "Saints preserve us. Could we have a quiet, non-crime spree, for the six weeks before the blessed event."

"Blessed event?" Dorie frowned at him. "It's a wedding, not a baby."

"What do you think happens next, girl?" Riley ducked as Dorie threw the new throw pillow at him. "Glad these are useful and not just decorative. I couldn't see the point when I bought my couch."

Ross groaned. "You should have taken Dorie with you."

"Are you two going to moan and groan or move the table and chairs in, so we can eat?" Dorie headed for the kitchen.

Riley whispered to Ross, "Now it begins."

About the Author

www.dianeetatumwriter.com
tatumlight@gmail.com

Diane E. Tatum began writing in grade school with short mystery stories, a play performed by her sixth-grade class, and a dictionary of supernatural beings. High school found her writing serial fiction with her friends, including developing characters and plot lines through hand-written notes. Her first book, *Gold Earrings,* is an outgrowth of a short story written in a high school creative writing class. This Main Street Mystery #2 follows #1 *Kudzu Sculptures*. Her writing list includes a 3-book series *Colonial Dream* and 2 contemporary romances

In addition to her writing career, Diane taught middle school language arts for 11 years. She has worked as a church youth group leader and worker since 1981. She currently serves as an adjunct professor of English at

Motlow State Community College.

She is loved and supported by her husband, Ken, and their two sons and daughters-in-law. Their four young grandsons are a joy to them all.

Books by Diane E. Tatum
Gold Earrings
Mission Mesquite
Oxford Fairy Tale
Colonial Dream, Book 1: A Time to Fight
Colonial Dream, Book 2: A Time to Love
Colonial Dream, Book 3: A Time to Choose
Main Street Mysteries: Kudzu Sculptures
Main Street Mysteries #2: The Gemini Conspiracy

Coming soon!
MISSletoe Romance: Wycroft Booksellers
Aphasia
Colonial Dream, Book 4: A Time to Create

If you enjoyed *Gemini Conspiracy*, please write a review on Amazon!

Bible Study/Book Discussion

Family. The ones with whom we share blood. The ones with whom we're related by marriage. The ones we choose for ourselves. The ones with whom we share the Holy Spirit. Often complicated. Sometimes difficult. Rarely easy. Even Jesus had family issues!

1. What issues does Riley have with his family? How does that lead to Ryker's rage? What other ways could Riley's family have handled the situation with the twins?

2. Ross becomes Riley's missing brother. How do friends become greater than family?

3. Dorie's family is far away. The people of Daelin are becoming her family. What characteristics make people 'family'?

4. Which friends have become your family? What characteristics do you expect of those friends who are your chosen family?

5. How do we choose our spouses? How do we deal with the rest of the in-laws?

6. Read Mark 3:20-21, 31-35. What does Jesus say about family?

7. Read Luke 9:57-62. What is Jesus saying about family versus the kingdom of heaven?

8. Read Luke 12:49-53. Does this sound like your family? What is Jesus trying to say?

9. Read Acts 7:9-14. Talk about a dysfunctional family! Where is the redemption in Joseph's family? In the story, how does Riley try to bring Ryker back to the family even though he has done heinous things to them?

10. Read Galatians 6:1-2, 7-10. Define 'doing good to all people' in light of our conversation about family.

11. Read Ephesians 3:2-6, 14-21. Jews and Gentiles in one family, in the grace of Jesus. Paul declares this to be a great mystery. Indeed, families are often hodgepodge mixtures of people, with different backgrounds, ideas, understandings. God's family may not agree on the color of carpet or to purchase a bus, but they are still family. How do you help God's family love one another?

12. Read 1 Thessalonians 4:9-12. How should we live as God's family?

13. Read 1 Timothy 5:3-5. Our blood family needs our help and respect, regardless of how crazy they make you feel sometimes! Caring for the elderly, the lonely, the ill or disabled is part of our responsibility as part of our family.

14. Read Hebrews 2:5-18. It is God through Jesus Christ that we have this holyamily of believers. How do we then live together in the bond of Christ?

15. Read 1 Peter 2:1-17. The family of God is the holy, royal priesthood. As His priests, we are called to live the Christian life before the world so they might be drawn to Him and redeemed. If we squabble among ourselves and do not show love to our spiritual family, how can we show Christ's love to the world?

16. Read 1 Peter 5:6-9. The church, as a family of believers, should not be fighting among ourselves. We have a greater enemy with whom we should be concerned. How does this speak to how we deal with our families, blood, relational, spiritual?

17. What do you think is the theme, the takeaway, from *Gemini Conspiracy*?

The first chapter from Mainstreet Mysteries #3, *Attic Visitations*

Chapter 1
Coming home from St. Louis …

Dorie Hudson and Ross MacAvoy pulled into the townhouse complex in Daelin, GA, after their Thanksgiving road trip to St. Louis. Ross had met Dorie's parents, and even better, they had approved of Ross as Dorie's fiancé. Wedding plans could begin in earnest now. Dorie was relieved but exhausted.

Riley McDonough rushed out into the parking lot to greet them. Riley was Ross's lifelong best friend, the closest Ross had to family. He was also Chief of Police to Daelin PD.

Riley gave Dorie a friendly hug. "How'd it go?"

Ross hopped out of the blue SUV. "Good. They like me."

"There was never any doubt." Dorie smiled at the broad shouldered, red-bearded, sandy-haired man she loved. "I just wanted them in the loop."

"Great. Now you guys can get married, so Ross can stop sleeping on my couch." Riley gave Ross a manly hug. "Let me help with the luggage."

"How'd you do over Thanksgiving, you know, without your mom?" Ross pulled his suitcase from the hatch. "What's the news about your twin Ryker and your dad?"

Riley shook his head. "Ryker took a plea deal for manslaughter and arson instead of murder. He's on his way to prison. Not sure about Lee. There's no statute of limitations for child support. I'm not holding my breath."

Ross walked over to Dorie at the driver's side. "You'd best get back to our house in Helen. It's late. I don't want you having a problem in the dark on the road up the mountain. The dog probably needs to stretch her legs too." He enfolded her in a hug.

Dorie melted in his embrace. "Darling, you need to be there too. Wedding soon?"

"It can't come soon enough, Sweetheart."

They kissed.

Dorie reluctantly released him. "Sleep well. I'll see you in the morning at Java Joint." She climbed into the SUV and started it up.

"Be safe." He reached in a touched her lips. "I love you."

She kissed his fingers. "I love you, too." She threw the car in gear and headed out.

Dorie unlocked the Helen house and released Star, her greyhound, to run through the house to the back door. She dropped her suitcase, coat, and backpack in the foyer.

"Hang on, girl, I'm coming to let you out." Dorie jogged through the house after Star and let her out in the backyard. She checked the gate was closed before turning around. Her gaze fell on something strange.

The lights in the kitchen were on. A dirty plate and glass sat on the bistro table. Lights were on upstairs as well. Dorie grabbed her backpack and Star's leash, quietly backed out of the house. She climbed into the SUV, then called 911. While she waited for the Helen PD to arrive, she wrangled Star out of the backyard on her leash and into the back of the SUV.

"I'm sorry, girl, I know it's been a long ride, but we

both need to be safe."

Then she called Ross. "Someone's been in the house."

"What do you mean?"

Dorie felt every nerve on edge. "Lights are on. Dirty dishes on the table. Someone's been in the house."

"I'm on my way. Sit tight in the car until the police arrive." He hung up.

Dorie watched the windows for some sign that 'Goldilocks' was still there. Her imagination had kicked into high gear, and she could see pretty much whatever she wanted. Was someone in the bedroom? Was that a light in the attic?

When the policeman's flashlight beamed in the window, she shrieked.

"I'm sorry." She recovered herself and stepped out of the vehicle. "I'm on edge."

"It's okay, Miss Dorie. We've gotten used to being here at Ross's house for one thing or another. What's up tonight?" The officer took pencil and incident pad out to take notes. "Dispatch said it was an intruder alert. Have you been in the house?"

"Yes, I took in my suitcase and my dog. I let her out. Then I noticed the lights were on, and there were dirty dishes in the kitchen." Dorie shivered, though it wasn't very cold. "Things were happening before we went to St. Louis. I thought it was my imagination with what was going on with Riley, Captain McDonough."

"You cleaned before you left then?"

"Well, no, not really. But I did put all the dishes away, and I turned off all the lights." A sense of being patronized seized her. "It is not my imagination."

"No one's saying that, ma'am. Just establishing the facts. Anyone else have a key?"

"Ross says no." As she spoke, Ross arrived in his grandpa's old truck. "Here he is now."

Ross joined her and the officer in the front yard. He wrapped an arm around her. "What's happening?"

"Nothing. He's just asking insulting questions." Dorie moved into his warmth and sulked.

The officer offered his hand, and Ross shook it.

"How's it going, Bobby?"

"New baby. No one's sleeping. That's about it." The officer grinned back at Ross.

Typical Ross. He knew pretty much everyone in Helen and Daelin. She'd only been there six months. It had become annoying to be the only one outside the loop.

"You stay here, Miss Dorie. Ross and I will check out the house." The officer was already walking away from her as he finished speaking.

Star began barking. Dorie got back into the SUV with her. "It's okay, baby, I'm here." Her head appeared over Dorie's shoulder. She petted Star's velvety fur as the men checked out the house. Star began to tick, a greyhound equivalent to a purr. She nuzzled Dorie's hair. Dorie wiped away anxious tears in frustration.

Finally, the men returned to the car. Dorie stepped out to hear their assessment.

"Well, Miss Dorie, I see the plate and cup. Are you sure you didn't forget to put them in the dishwasher before you left?"

Dorie huffed. "No, sir. I didn't leave dishes on the table."

"Okay. We'll see if we can get any prints off them." Bobby sealed a Ziplock bag, probably from her own kitchen, with the plate and glass in it.

"What about the light switches?" The knot in Dorie's chest tightened. "Aren't you going to fingerprint them?"

"When did you last wipe down your light switches, ma'am?" The officer, Bobby, gave her a sideways look.

"Never. I've only lived here three months."

"Exactly. Unlikely we'll get any kind of print that matters on them."

Ross stepped toward her and gathered her to him. "Relax, sweetheart. It's okay. No one is here now."

"And he thinks I'm a lousy housekeeper and a liar with memory problems."

"No, ma'am. I don't think nothing like that. I just know that after a long trip, people are afraid to find their house not right. Sometimes people are just tired. Y'know?"

"I can stay the night on the couch if it would make you feel better." Ross squeezed her closer. "Would that help?"

Dorie looked from Ross to the police officer. "Fine."

"Good. I'll be going then." Bobby slammed his incident book closed. "Y'all try to get some sleep." Then he winked at Ross. "If you can, that is." He walked to the squad car and drove away.

Dorie pulled away from Ross and hit him in the arm. "You let him be condescending, sexist, and implying you were going to take advantage of the situation. How could you?"

She reached into the SUV and grabbed Star's leash. Star bounded out and danced around them. Dorie stalked toward the gate and let Star off her leash to run the backyard. Security lights came on as Star ran past them.

***

Dorie went into the house while Ross began emptying the car of Star's crate and essentials. He also grabbed Dorie's bag that she'd left in the front seat. He loved her, but she did not like men to treat her like a silly woman. Of course, he knew she was pretty much brilliant as well as beautiful. She was also a spitfire when men underestimated her. Ross knew better than that.

Guess it was another night on the futon. Was that better than the couch at Riley's? Of course, it was. He'd

191

be in his own house with his forever love upstairs. Once they were married, he wasn't sleeping on that futon ever again. He had to dump it since they bought a new couch.